"You're all I have."

Despite Reyna's words, his patience neared the breaking point. "Tell me who they are."

"I don't know." Then she slumped forward, as if she couldn't take any more. "They came to my house and threatened me. They said my husband had taken something they wanted. Jase, I think these men killed him. And now they're after me. We need to get out of here."

The noise of approaching vehicles grew louder. As much as he needed to know more about the danger she'd brought to his door, if they didn't leave soon there would be no way out.

He led her into the night. "Take my hand. We can't risk using the flashlight. Stay quiet. Noise carries for miles up in these mountains."

She clasped his hand. The tremors in her gave away her fear, and his heart went out to her.

It might be the worst mistake of his life, but he believed everything she'd told him. He'd do whatever it took to protect his friend's widow...or he would die trying.

Mary Alford was inspired to become a writer after reading romantic suspense greats Victoria Holt and Phyllis Whitney. Soon, creating characters and throwing them into dangerous situations that test their faith came naturally for Mary. In 2012 Mary entered the Speed Dating contest hosted by Love Inspired Suspense and later received "the call." Writing for Love Inspired Suspense has been a dream come true for Mary.

Books by Mary Alford

Love Inspired Suspense

Forgotten Past
Rocky Mountain Pursuit

Visit the Author Profile page at Harlequin.com.

ROCKY MOUNTAIN PURSUIT

MARY ALFORD

⬥**HARLEQUIN**® LOVE INSPIRED® SUSPENSE

Recycling programs for this product may not exist in your area.

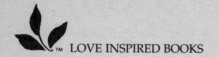 LOVE INSPIRED BOOKS

ISBN-13: 978-0-373-44723-7

Rocky Mountain Pursuit

Copyright © 2016 by Mary Eason

This edition published by arrangement with Love Inspired Books.

® and TM are trademarks of Love Inspired Books, used under license. Trademarks indicated with ® are registered in the United States Patent and Trademark Office, the Canadian Intellectual Property Office and in other countries.

www.Harlequin.com

Printed in U.S.A.

But they that wait upon the Lord shall renew their strength;
they shall mount up with wings as eagles; they shall run,
and not be weary; and they shall walk, and not faint.
—Isaiah 40:31

To the men and women of our armed forces
who risk their lives daily so that we might
enjoy the freedom that we do today.
Thank you from the bottom of my heart for your sacrifice.

PROLOGUE

A thunderous rap on her front door jerked Dr. Reyna Peterson's attention from the letter she'd been reading seconds earlier. Her heart slammed against her chest at the ominous tone of the knock. It was almost eleven at night and she wasn't expecting company so late.

The pounding grew louder and more demanding. Whoever was out there wasn't going away. Reyna shoved the letter into the pocket of her robe, flipped on the outside light and inched the curtains apart. Three extremely menacing-looking men dressed in suits stood on her front porch. She didn't recognize any of them.

If it weren't for the unsettling contents of Eddie's letter warning her this moment might come, Reyna might not have thought anything unusual about the men on her porch. But now, coupled with the events leading up to her husband's death, she wasn't so sure.

She glanced around the living room as the banging was followed by an angry voice, demanding, "Open the door, Dr. Peterson. Now. Federal agents."

Don't trust anyone from the government, Eddie had warned in the letter.

The door rattled in someone's grasp. Were they going to break the door down? Her chest constricted with fear.

Reyna grabbed the phone to call 9-1-1, but what the man said next had her ending the call before she placed it.

"This is about your husband, Dr. Peterson, and what he stole from his country. If you don't want to be charged as a coconspirator to treason, I suggest you open the door."

Every instinct inside of her warned against it, but in her heart she knew she had to find out what they were accusing Eddie of stealing, because she had a feeling she knew already.

"Please, Lord, protect me," she whispered under her breath. Her fingers shook as she slowly unlocked the dead bolt. Before she could open the door, the men burst inside without invitation. The door hit Reyna in the shoulder and sent her stumbling backward. She almost lost her footing.

Now she was truly terrified. Three strange men were in her house and she was alone.

"What do you think you're doing? You can't just barge in here without invitation—"

"We can," interrupted the man who had spoken earlier. He was obviously the leader.

"Who are you?" Her voice wobbled over every syllable. Truth be told, she was shaking all over. Their intimidating stance petrified her and they were obviously armed. She could see a gun tucked inside the leader's jacket.

He dug in his pocket and pulled out a badge. "Agent Martin. Intelligence." He flashed it briefly in her face, but she was so rattled she didn't have time to read his name much less verify the details he'd given her.

"It's late, Agent Martin. Why are you here?"

He moved threateningly closer and into her personal space. Reyna took an involuntary step backward and the edge of his mouth quirked upward in obvious satisfaction. "I told you this is about your husband."

"My husband is dead…"

Agent Martin's steely glare showed no reaction. "Your husband is dead because of his allegiance to a terrorist organization. Your husband was a traitor."

His words struck like blows. "That's not true!" she exclaimed.

The smug grin on Agent Martin's face confirmed he had something to back up those words. "I assure you it is. Peterson took a laptop containing highly confidential government documents and we want it back."

He motioned to the two men with him and they began searching the room, tossing her personal possessions everywhere.

Reyna couldn't believe what was happening. "What are you doing? You have no right to search my home without my permission."

The men continued with the search as if she hadn't spoken.

"Not only do we have the right to search your house and confiscate anything suspicious, we also have the authority to take you into custody without giving you so much as the privilege of a phone call if you don't cooperate. Do you want to be charged as a traitor?"

Reyna struggled to draw air into her lungs.

"Where's the laptop, Dr. Peterson?" Agent Martin asked impatiently. "I'm sure your husband told you where he hid it. We need it now—otherwise, I can only assume you are as guilty as he."

"I don't know what you're talking about." But she did. Eddie's letter had detailed where she should go to find the laptop. It had been by God's hand that she'd received the letter from Eddie's father that very afternoon. Ed Sr. told her he'd found it tucked away in a drawer with a note informing him to send it to Reyna if something were to happen to Eddie.

Agent Martin practically snarled at her in response as the two men rejoined them once more. They shook their heads.

Martin moved closer, inches from her face, his eyes seething with anger. "Enough games. Tell me where it is, Doctor. I'd hate to have to haul you in to make you talk. We have ways of getting information out of people and I promise you won't like it."

She shivered at his all-out threat. He wasn't even trying to hide it now.

"Believe me, Doctor, these charges are real, and you're going to want to get in front of them if you ever hope to have the chance at seeing the light of day outside of a prison cell."

As she looked up at him, Reyna realized she didn't trust anything he said. There was more going on here than what Agent Martin was telling her.

"I don't have a laptop and you're wrong about my husband. Eddie wasn't a traitor. He loved his country…" She stopped when the two men came and stood behind her. She could feel their hot breath on her neck. They were going to arrest her.

"You're lying." Agent Martin surmised as he continued to pin her with his gaze.

Reyna lifted her chin. "No, I'm not." Her fingers rested on the letter in her pocket, confirming that Eddie did at one time possess the laptop in question. If they searched her and found it, they'd make good on their promises and she might never have the chance to prove her husband's innocence. "I know my rights, Agent Martin, and I happen to still have friends at the CIA.

They'll come looking for me. You can't arrest me without charging me." She silently prayed he didn't call her bluff. After a handful of seconds ticked by in a silent standoff, Agent Martin finally nodded to the two men behind her and they strode over to the door.

"You have two days to bring us the laptop, Doctor. Otherwise, we'll be back and you'll face the consequences. Serving a life sentence for treason will be the least of your worries."

Agent Martin slammed the door behind him and Reyna rushed over and slid the dead bolt back into place. She slumped against the door and onto the floor, her legs no longer able to support her.

After she drew in a handful of calming breaths, she could think clearly once more. She needed help. The type of help Eddie had explained in his letter. *If anything happens to me—if they come for you and threaten you—go to Defiance, Colorado. Find my former colleague, Jase Bradford.*

But finding Jase Bradford was going to prove a near impossible task since he'd supposedly died from his battle injuries three years earlier—in spite of Eddie's insistence that Jase wasn't actually dead.

Reyna killed the lights, crawled over to the window and glanced outside. A black Suburban was parked down the street from her house. They weren't leaving. They were going to watch and see if she led them to the laptop. She couldn't let that happen.

She got to her feet and raced to her bedroom. Taking down her old suitcase, she threw as much stuff as she could fit into it and then slipped out the back door. She didn't dare risk using her vehicle. They'd be looking for it. She'd have to borrow her neighbor and good friend Sara Dawson's car if she stood any chance of staying out of prison long enough to retrieve the laptop and find Jase Bradford.

As Reyna walked out into the humid Texas night, it scared the daylights out of her to think that she was risking her freedom, if not her life, on locating a man who the entire world believed was dead.

ONE

Reyna's breath stuck in her throat. She clutched the steering wheel in a death grip to try to keep the tiny car from sliding off the ice-encrusted road. She was way out of her comfort zone. Truth be told, she had been since the nightmare first began.

She slowed to a snail's pace as an onslaught of ice and snow clung to the windshield, making visibility next to zero. The storm had continued to intensify since she'd been up on the mountain. She had never felt more terrified or alone than she did at this moment, yet turning back wasn't an option. Behind her lay almost certain prison time—or worse. Agent Martin had all but promised as much. Still, no matter what lay ahead, she had to find out the truth. Was Jase Bradford dead or alive? Reyna believed her life might depend on the answer.

Her eyes darted fearfully to the rearview mirror. What if the men watching her house had somehow managed to follow her here to Defiance, Colorado? She couldn't let them find the laptop and then kill her before she had the chance to clear Eddie's name and prove her husband had been murdered. To keep that from happening Reyna had devised a plan. After she'd called the hospital to let her supervisor know she would be taking an extended leave of absence, she had left the laptop in a secure storage facility in Eldorado, Colorado. Then she'd sent a letter to Sara letting her know where to find it if something were to happen to her.

Reyna scrubbed her hand over her weary eyes. The frantic thirteen-plus-hour drive from Stevens, Texas, to Defiance had taken its toll. She was exhausted beyond belief. Thinking clearly took more strength than she had. She'd hit Defiance a couple of hours before darkness descended and just as the edge of the storm arrived.

Maggie, the woman working the night shift at the diner, told her there were only four houses up on Defiance Mountain and none of them belonged to a Jase Bradford. Still, Reyna pressed on because she was all out of options. She believed Eddie had been murdered for what he'd discovered on the laptop. If she wanted to stay out of prison long enough to prove that, then she'd need Jase Bradford's help to unravel the contents of the files hidden there.

Reyna leaned forward in her seat. She'd driven past three of the houses already and there were clear signs no one had been home in quite some time. One house remained. The last one up was almost at the top of the mountain, according to Maggie, and the storm wasn't showing any sign of letting up.

She could now barely see the hood of the car, much less the road. The conditions were deteriorating quickly and she had no idea how much farther the car could make it.

Even facing all those dangers, her biggest fear was that Eddie had been wrong and the man buried in Arlington National Cemetery was indeed Jase Bradford. After all, they both had attended his memorial service at Langley. Everyone including the CIA acknowledged Jase was dead.

Why then had Eddie been so convinced in the weeks before *his* death that Jase was still alive?

She eased down on the gas pedal and the tires spun on the slick gravel, spewing debris against the underside of the car. Since she'd moved from DC back to her childhood home, Reyna had grown accustomed to mild winters. Nothing in Stevens, Texas, had prepared her for this.

The tires finally caught, the car lurched forward, and Reyna remembered to breathe. The road continued its upward spiral broken only by a series of switchbacks that snaked around the side of the mountain. Her heartbeat pounded a frantic rhythm in her ears when she reached another ninety-degree bend. She'd been at it for over an hour and had only managed a quarter of a mile.

Up ahead, the headlights flashed across the left side the road. It appeared to slough off a good foot from the edge. It was pitch-black out and she had no idea how steep the drop-off was. A fall would almost certainly result in major injuries…or death. If she did survive, hypothermia would set in quickly. She'd be dead by morning.

Reyna nudged the car along. She had almost reached the end of the switchback when she felt the vehicle slide on black ice and inch closer to the side of the mountain. Panicking, she jerked the wheel hard in the opposite direction. The small car skated backward some twenty feet. As a result, the tires lost their tenuous grip and slithered closer to the edge.

She floored the gas and the vehicle wrenched forward, swerved sideways and headed straight for the drop-off. Reyna screamed and tried to turn the wheel but it was useless. It moved freely in her hands. She had lost control.

Reyna closed her eyes and prayed with all her heart. She didn't want to die up here. Not alone like this. Not without proving Eddie's innocence.

"Please, Lord, no."

The car spun 360 degrees a couple of times until the front tires slipped over the edge of the mountain and were suspended in midair. The car rocked a couple of times and then stopped. Reyna slowly reached for the door handle. If she could just open the door, she could leap out before it was too late.

She tentatively lifted the handle; the vehicle tilted back and forth from the simple movement. An eerie silence surrounded her. The car hung in place for a second longer and then tipped forward. Reyna barely had time to scream again before the tiny car hurled itself headfirst over the side of the mountain.

Davis Sinclair stomped hard on the brakes of his battered SUV and somehow managed to keep from spinning out on the slippery road. The first storm of the season had hit hard and fast. It was barely September and already the storm had dumped a foot of snow in a matter of hours. It had piled up on the gravel road leading to his house.

He had been so focused on getting back home through the wintry mix that he hadn't noticed the skid marks on the road until he was right on top of them.

Someone else had been up his mountain.

The new-fallen snow covered most of their tracks. Still, he hadn't become aware of them until now, and that concerned him most of all. He was slipping. He'd been gone from the CIA too long.

A familiar fear coiled deep in the pit of his stomach. There would be no reason for anyone to come this far up the mountain. Especially in these conditions.

Davis squinted through the cracked windshield at the skid marks that started about twenty feet in front of him. That wasn't the part that worried him. It was the direction they were heading. Straight off the side of the mountain.

Was this just some innocent traveler lost in the storm, or the moment he'd feared for three years?

His heart drummed in his ears as he grabbed a flashlight along with his Glock and shoved the Jeep's door open against the howling wind. The freezing air mixed with sleet robbed him of his breath. Instinct had him panning the area for unseen trouble. Was it a setup? Had his identity been blown? It could be someone dead set on eliminating the threat he still posed. Old habits died hard. Three years, and he still hadn't broken his.

He shook off the past with effort and trudged through the additional snow that had fallen since he'd left home.

The flashlight's beam picked up a small car perched about ten feet over the edge. Another three feet to the left and the car would be halfway down the mountain by now. As it was, it had laid bare a five-foot-wide stretch of dirt once covered in heavy brush and small trees, before coming to rest in a grove of aspens.

Davis shoved the Glock inside his jacket pocket, braced his right foot against one of the mangled tree trunks and shone the flashlight's beam on the ground. Putting one foot against available trunks and another on an exposed rock, he slowly made his way down to the car.

He could see the driver—a woman—leaning forward in her seat, her head almost touching the steering wheel, the seat belt the only thing keeping her upright. The airbag hadn't deployed. He couldn't tell if she was dead or alive.

He yanked at the door. The woman moaned and Davis breathed a sigh of relief.

"Are you hurt?" he asked her, and watched as she struggled to focus on him. He noticed a quarter-sized red spot on her forehead that had the makings of one nasty bruise.

Davis moved closer and she shrank away, terror written on every inch of her face.

"No," she said at last. "I don't think so. It happened so quickly. I thought I had made the turn and then…" She fumbled with her seat belt.

"Hang on a second. Don't try to move until we're sure you're not hurt."

She didn't listen and, instead, scrambled to undo her restraint. The woman was obviously suffering from shock.

The latch freed and Davis caught her before she could fall forward. His arm circled her waist and she froze. He lifted her out of the car and set her on her feet. The moment she was safely on ground, she pushed his hands away and distanced herself from him. It was clear he made her nervous.

The storm around them was no comparison to the one raging in her startling emerald green eyes. It had been a long time since he'd seen such panic. Was it just because of her near-death experience or fueled by something more?

Her light brown hair, once tied into a ponytail, was now mostly escaping. The first thing to strike him as unusual was that she seemed familiar. Impossible. They'd never met before; he was almost certain of it.

Davis realized he was staring and quickly pulled himself together. Too much time spent alone, obviously. "We need to get you out of here. The storm's not easing any. Can you walk?"

She took a tentative step forward. "Yes, I think so."

"Good."

He gazed up at the sky. The weather conditions were definitely worsening and he had a decision to make. He couldn't leave her here and the car didn't appear drivable. But there was another option. He could take her back into town and deposit her at the hotel then wait out the rest of the snowstorm from Maggie's Diner.

His was the only house past the last curve. No one came this far up the mountain by accident. So what brought her here? Old fears from his past life slowly crept in. She didn't appear to be a threat, but he'd learned the hard way not to depend on appearances. Bad people came in innocent-looking packages, and in the spy business, you never let down your guard.

"What were you doing up here on the mountain in this storm anyway?" he asked through narrowed eyes, carefully gauging her reaction.

"I'm...searching for someone."

Her body language told him she wasn't being completely honest and he needed answers.

"There's no one up here but me, so let's try this again. Who are you and why are you really here?"

Her gaze collided with his, and he lost his equilibrium for a second. Even scared to death and as cagey as a trapped bear, she had the type of beauty that took his breath away. He hadn't thought of another woman in such a way since Abby, and it bothered him that a total stranger could illicit such thoughts.

"My name is Reyna Peterson and I have told you the

truth," she retorted, bristling at his tone. "I am trying to find someone. A friend of my husband's."

She was married. A simple gold band on her left hand seemed to confirm her story, but he couldn't let go of the doubts. "Oh yeah? What's the friend's name?"

She hesitated, evidently torn between answering his question and keeping her secrets. His internal radar pegged the top of the chart.

She cleared her throat. "Jase Bradford. His name is Jase Bradford."

Shock and disbelief threatened to buckle his knees. He hadn't heard that name in years. He had long ago buried the person he'd been back then.

Somehow, Davis managed to get coherent words to come out of his mouth. "There's no one by that name around these parts. Your husband is mistaken." A hard edge crept into his tone as it always did whenever he thought about the past.

Reyna stared at him in a way that conveyed she either didn't believe him or didn't want to.

"Eddie was so sure I would find him here..." she murmured, almost to herself.

Eddie. Eddie *Peterson*? No, not possible. He couldn't have heard right. "Your husband's name is...Eddie?" He latched on to the name as a distraction because it felt as if someone had slugged him hard in the chest. With the exception of his former handler, Kyle Jennings, Eddie was the last remaining member of the Scorpion team still alive. Eddie wouldn't be trying to make contact with him without good cause. And why send his wife? Had something happened to his former comrade?

"Yes," she confirmed reluctantly. The second the words were out, he could see she thought better of sharing them. "I'm sorry. None of this is your problem."

She had no idea how wrong she was. Eddie Peterson had been one of his own. He'd recruited him personally as part of the elite Scorpion team after the failed weapons mission near Tora Bora had taken the lives of two crucial team members. Eddie had been a good fit with the team and they'd grown close while serving side by side. Her husband *was* his problem. And now so was she.

Davis's plans had now changed. Instead of going back to Defiance, he'd take her to his place. See what he could find out by morning. Pray that all of this would turn out to be just some strange coincidence and then send her on her way. Unfortunately, he didn't believe in coincidences. Especially ones this huge.

A deluge of wintry mix pelted his face like tiny bullets and his feet were numb. "There's no way to get your car out of here tonight." He crooked a thumb in the direction of his SUV. "My ride's just up there. Let's get you warm. You're shivering. I can come back and get whatever you need for the night and we'll deal with the car in the morning."

Reyna didn't budge. He could see she didn't trust him. Not the normal reaction of someone just rescued from almost certain death.

"We'll be stuck up here if we stay much longer," he added, hoping to convince her.

She hesitated another second before giving in. "You're right. We need to get out of the storm. It's got to be well below freezing out here."

Try as he might, he couldn't get a good read off her, and he didn't like it. Not one bit. "Watch your step."

She clutched the edge of his jacket in a vise grip as she followed close behind, slipping over the icy mess.

Davis reached for her hand to help her the last bit

of the way up to the road. The touch of her hand in his sparked a sweet memory of Abby from long ago. They had slipped away for a few brief moments alone between missions. They'd climbed a snowcapped mountain in Afghanistan and spent the afternoon together, just enjoying the breathtaking view and the quiet they'd found amid a raging war.

Back then he'd still believed love was possible. That was before he'd lost Abby. He shoved that painful memory deep within the dark recesses of his broken heart.

Through the swirling storm, he located the Jeep and they trudged through deep snow the short distance. He forced open the passenger door and waited while she climbed inside.

Davis went around to the driver's side, got in and cranked the heater up another notch. Reyna was shaking uncontrollably. He grabbed a blanket from the backseat and wrapped it around her shoulders.

For the first time she smiled and it caught him completely off guard. She had a pretty smile. It eased some of the tautness from around her mouth and eyes.

"Thank you for saving me," she whispered. "If you hadn't come along when you did, I—I wouldn't have made it. With the temperature dropping so quickly and prolonged exposure to the elements, hypothermia doesn't take long to set in…" He gave her a quizzical look and she laughed. "Sorry, I'm sure you must know all about the dangers of exposure living up here. I'm a doctor," she explained. "Sometimes it's hard to shut it off."

He absorbed this new piece of information with a nod. He remembered something Eddie had said once about his wife studying to be a pediatric surgeon. That part seemed to lend credence to her story.

"My place is a couple of miles farther up the road. You can spend the night there. In the morning, I'll see if I can get the car unstuck." Her smile disappeared. Apparently, the thought of being alone with him made her uneasy. She glanced nervously behind them as if she was looking for someone. He had to find out what she was hiding.

"I promise you'll be safe there," he added somberly.

"Okay," she finally agreed, and he let out a breath he hadn't realized he'd been holding.

"Good. Tell me what you need from the car." He continued to analyze her reactions very carefully and came to the conclusion she wasn't an assassin. She gave too much away. Still, the odds of Eddie's wife showing up on his mountain without a dire reason were just too high to ignore.

Reyna sat up a little straighter in her seat. "There's a tote bag. It was in the front seat next to me. It has… my purse and phone."

There was something more in the bag she needed. He saw its significance before she could camouflage it.

"Why don't you stay here where it's warm and I'll go get it?" He didn't wait for her answer, mostly because he had no intention of taking her with him. He wanted to find out what was so important in the bag that couldn't wait until morning.

Davis turned up the collar of his jacket and braced to battle the cold.

The moment he left the safety of the Jeep, a torrent bombarded him, drenching his clothing straight through to his skin. He slipped and slid his way down the side of the mountain until he finally reached the car once more. He found the bag in question lying on the floorboard of the passenger seat.

A quick search produced a prepaid phone. Why would she need one of those unless she was trying to keep her location secret? He dug further and found a small plastic bear key chain with several keys attached and a woman's purse below that. Inside the purse were a few fast-food receipts and a wallet.

He pulled out her wallet and opened it. A Texas driver's license with her name on it, a handful of tens and a couple of credit cards. An access ID card from Stevens Memorial Hospital confirmed what she did for a living. In the coin purse, he found another key that looked as if it could fit any storage locker. Not much to go on. Still, he didn't like it. Three years and not a peep from his past until tonight.

The remoteness of the area was the very reason Davis had moved back to Defiance. No one from his childhood lived here anymore. The Defiance Silver Mine, the main source of employment for the area, closed down about fifteen years earlier and the town had all but dried up. When he'd left his old identity behind, Kyle had destroyed his CIA personnel file. There would be no record of his past life anywhere. Other than Kyle, no one from the Agency knew he had grown up in Defiance.

With the exception of Eddie.

It finally dawned on Davis why Reyna looked so familiar. Eddie had shown him a picture of his wife once. He was so proud of her. Eddie told him that Reyna's parents had died when she was barely a teenager. Lots of kids would have fallen apart after losing their entire family. Not Reyna. If anything, it had made her stronger. Eddie said that after they'd gotten married she'd held down two jobs just to put herself through medical school.

Davis did a quick search of the rest of the contents of the car and found nothing out of the ordinary. A suitcase laden with clothing and toiletries indicated she'd planned for a long period away from home. She was running from someone. Eddie? It didn't add up. Everything he knew about the man pointed to someone who wasn't violent. Besides, she'd said she was looking for her husband's friend, which seemed to imply Eddie had sent her.

On impulse, he dumped the contents of the suitcase on the seat and found what he was after. A small box that contained a set of dog tags. Eddie's. There would be only one reason the tags would leave a soldier's body. If he were killed in action.

Eddie Peterson was dead.

Shocked, Davis slumped back against the seat, covering his face with his hands. Grief and disbelief made it hard to draw air into his lungs. He couldn't wrap his mind around the knowledge his friend was dead.

"Why, God? Why Eddie? He was an innocent," he said in a broken tone and struggled to hold back the tears.

Eddie hadn't been part of the original Scorpion team that was being targeted for death, so Davis had believed him safe.

Why hadn't Kyle contacted him about Eddie? His friend knew how close he and Eddie had become. He didn't like it. Something was wrong. Davis believed if it were humanly possible, Kyle would have reached out to him about Eddie. The fact that he hadn't didn't bode well.

The threat facing the original Scorpions had been real enough for Davis to fake his death. Kyle was probably in grave danger, too, since he was the handler for the group. Had Kyle gone into hiding himself or...was he dead?

"Please, God, no." Losing Eddie was gut wrenching enough. He didn't want to think about the possibility of Kyle being dead, too.

Both Davis and Kyle had long believed something the Scorpions had witnessed during their time in the Tora Bora region was the real reason behind their systematic annihilation. But Eddie hadn't been part of those missions. He'd joined the team later on.

A surge of guilt shot through Davis, catapulting him back three years to that horrific day when his life had changed forever.

Sometimes at night, he could still hear the firefight exploding around him. See the smoke and the flames. On those really bad nights, he could feel the bullet searing through his flesh as it destroyed his leg.

That night, well, it had had given him the reason he needed to get out of the CIA, especially after learning the woman he loved had perished in the same battle. His injuries had been severe enough to send him home. But Abby and so many others had sacrificed their lives.

Nowadays, the physical wounds were all but gone. The only reminder was a limp and the occasional throbbing ache when bad weather moved in. Like today. But the emotional wounds he carried inside ran much deeper. No matter how much he prayed for release, he doubted if he'd ever be done with them entirely.

Davis let go of those dark memories with difficulty. What was the point of reliving what he couldn't change? He'd gotten good at stuffing his feelings down inside. Only sometimes, on occasion, they refused to stay buried. When that happened, he dove into his Bible and prayed for God's help.

Releasing a ragged breath, he got to his feet and put the tags back in the suitcase then threw the clothes over them. He'd do a more thorough search in the morning. Right now, he needed to get Eddie's wife out of here and to safety.

Davis grabbed the tote bag and hiked back up to the SUV. He stopped at the edge of the road. He could see Reyna hunkered down inside. She had leaned back against the headrest, her eyes shut. He remembered the picture Eddie showed him. His buddy had told him they took it right after they were married. Davis remembered thinking how pretty she looked back then, and how innocent. Reyna Peterson had grown from a shy-looking bride into a strikingly beautiful and accomplished woman.

Still, something had left an indelible mark on her. She appeared weary from life. No doubt partly due to Eddie's death, but there had to be more to her story. Her skittish behavior only reinforced that feeling.

Davis jerked the driver's door open with a little more force than necessary. Reyna jumped as if he'd startled her and her hand flew to her chest. "Sorry. I didn't mean to frighten you." He handed her the bag and she clutched it against her body like a life support. Further proof that the value of its contents were of grave importance to her.

Davis put the Jeep into Drive. The wipers slapped back and forth at high speed, trying to fend off the ice and snow blanketing the windshield.

"How much farther?" she asked, continuing to watch the passenger mirror.

He glanced her way. "Not much. A couple more miles. Are you expecting company?"

Her gaze flew to his and he saw the truth before she could deny it. His nerves hit the critical mark. Was someone following her?

The Jeep crept along the road, occasionally slipping as the snow chains struggled to hold their grip. Each time he sensed she was trying not to scream.

"Why do you need to find this Jase Bradford fellow? Where's your husband?" So far, she didn't have a clue Davis was the one she was looking for. He planned to keep it that way. He'd find out what she needed, do his best to help her for Eddie's sake, then send her on her way before someone realized he was still alive.

Reyna edged a little farther away, as if his questions made her uncomfortable. "That's none of your business."

His mouth quirked up in a grin. "I think you kind of made it my business, don't you?"

She shot him an annoyed look, then stared straight ahead. "My husband is dead." She confirmed the news of Eddie's fate with those simple words.

It was a long time before Davis could bring forth a steady answer over the lump in his throat. "I'm sorry. That must have been difficult. How long?"

She swallowed visibly. "Six months. It's been six months and I still can't wrap my head around it. We were best friends forever. We went through most of our school years together." Her voice caught and he could see tears in her eyes. "There are times when I still expect him to walk through the door."

Davis understood what she was going through all too well. He felt the same way about Abby. They'd worked side by side together for more than six years. He'd loved her just as long. When he'd learned of her death he'd fallen apart. It didn't seem possible that such a vibrant, strong woman could be gone. At times, during those lonely winter nights when the walls closed in, he let himself think about the future they might have had. An impossible dream now.

"You know, I was so grateful you stopped to help that I completely forgot to ask your name," Reyna said.

His breath stuck in his throat, his composure all but shot. For a second, he debated giving her another of his aliases, but thought better of it. "It's Davis," he said, without looking at her.

"Davis what?" she prodded.

His expression hardened. "Davis Sinclair," he said at last. "Satisfied?"

"Yes. Sorry, it's just…been a very bad day."

Bad day? He thought it was much more than that. "You still haven't answered *my* question. Why is it so important you find this Bradford guy?"

She took her time answering. Something in her beautiful, fragile countenance tore at his heart. It made him want to protect her. In spite of that, he killed the remnant of emotion before it could take hold. He couldn't go there. He'd do what he could to help her for Eddie's sake.

And then he'd move on.

"Eddie told me if I was ever…if I ever needed help, I could trust Jase Bradford."

Had she been about to say if she was ever in danger? Was someone threatening Reyna because of her relationship to Eddie?

His hands tightened on the wheel. "And what if you don't locate this guy? What then?"

The sheer desperation on her face confirmed failure wasn't an option.

"What did your husband tell you about this man? Do you even know what he looks like?" Davis added brusquely when she didn't answer. He was on a fishing expedition of his own. He wanted to know what Eddie had told her about *him*. She obviously knew where to find him.

He steeled himself when she shot him another piercing glance. *Did* she know what he looked like? No way. He'd changed his appearance dramatically. Let his hair grow. Years of working outdoors had lightened his dirty-blond hair somewhat. He'd even managed to grow a beard. He'd traded his fatigues for plaids and jeans. The only part of his previous uniform he still possessed was the Glock stashed in his pocket.

"I know Jase Bradford was born here in Defiance and at one time his family lived up this same mountain. And I have a photo."

"A photo?" Davis's heart lurched as he pulled the Jeep in front of the gate and stopped abruptly. There was no way she had a photo of him. In their line of work, anonymity was crucial. You couldn't afford to have your picture floating around where it could quite possibly fall into enemy hands.

"Why are we stopping?" she asked nervously.

As desperate as he was to find out more about the photo, he didn't want to tip his hand just yet. He needed to tread carefully.

He pointed to the locked gate in front of them. "I need to open it. I'll be right back."

Davis took his time. His usually tough composure had taken a beating when she mentioned a photo, and he struggled to regain his footing. His life might depend on it.

TWO

Reyna watched the man who had come to her rescue throw open the gate with enough force to send it rocking on its hinges. She glanced around at her surroundings. The isolation of the place sent up all sorts of warning signals. Had she behaved foolishly in trusting a complete stranger whose motives were unclear?

She'd been so intent in finding Jase Bradford that she hadn't fully thought her actions through. Now all the odd behavior Eddie had displayed before he left on that final tour of duty came back to taunt her. Could her original diagnosis have been correct all along? Maybe Eddie *had* been suffering from PTSD, as she'd first believed, and Jase Bradford was truly dead.

But even if Eddie had been ill, that still didn't explain why Agent Martin and his goons had shown up at her house and accused Eddie of treason. She'd known the moment they barged in that something was terribly wrong, and so she'd run.

Reyna had done her best to cover her tracks. She hadn't taken a direct route to Defiance, but had made several deliberate stops along the way, including the one to the storage facility in Eldorado. All designed to throw off a possible tail. She was almost positive no one had followed her. Almost.

Still, as the miles had disappeared behind her, the terror and paranoia had grown. Lack of sleep had a way playing on a person's uncertainties. She couldn't give in to them. The first thing she'd done when she arrived in Defiance was to call her friend Sara with the disposable phone she'd purchased along the way. Sara had been worried sick when Reyna showed up at her back door and asked to borrow her car. She had begged Reyna to tell her what was happening, but Reyna knew it was best she didn't know about the threat. She hadn't told Sara about the letter containing the location of the storage facility, either. She had put her friend's life in enough jeopardy simply by association.

Now she wondered if she'd made a terrible mistake by not taking Sara up on her offer to help. She'd simply run off on her own and ended up in the middle of nowhere with a man she knew nothing about. He could be a serial killer. Or worse. Working for the same thugs who she believed had killed Eddie and threatened her.

Reyna braced herself as Davis headed back to the Jeep…and then she saw it. She leaned forward in her seat in amazement. He had a limp! She hadn't noticed it before, but then she'd just gone through a traumatic experience. Now that she thought about it, she vividly recalled the days following Eddie's return stateside after the attack on the team. Eddie had been in shock. He'd told her that with the exception of Jase, Kyle and himself, the entire team had died. Eddie believed it was a deliberate attack on the unit that had nothing to do with the mission they were on.

Her husband told her Jase's injuries were extensive. A bullet had shattered his right leg. Another one had punctured his lung. He'd been flown to a military hospital near DC. She and Eddie had received news from

Kyle of Jase's passing a few days later. Yet, even after they attended the memorial service at Langley, Reyna could tell Eddie didn't believe his friend was dead. In the weeks prior to Eddie's own death, he'd insisted Jase had had no choice but to fake his death.

If Jase had survived, as Eddie believed, then he definitely would have a limp. Reyna dug into her jacket pocket and pulled out the photo she'd hidden there. It showed all the Scorpion team members. The man she knew to be Jase Bradford was slightly younger in the photo and clean shaven. Still, the resemblance was uncanny. It certainly was plausible that Davis Sinclair could be Jase Bradford.

She wasn't sure what she had been expecting to feel. If Bradford was alive, then everything else Eddie told her must be the truth. The thought alone was chilling.

Reyna quickly tucked the photo away before Davis got into the Jeep and turned to her. His gaze narrowed as he watched her try to recover from the incredible shock of learning the person seated next to her might quite possibly be a dead man.

"Anything wrong?" he asked.

She pulled in a shaky breath, her survival instincts cautioning her to watch what she said. "No, I'm fine."

He accepted her answer with a curt nod and put the vehicle in gear.

Once he'd relocked the gate, he drove past snow-covered trees lining both sides of the drive. They rounded a ninety-degree curve and the house appeared before them. The hair on her arms stood to attention and she shivered. Nothing about the place was inviting.

"This is it," he said as he eased the car to a stop. "Hang on just a second, I'll come around and help you. There's ice everywhere." He shoved his door open and got out. The noise stretched her raw nerves closer to the breaking point.

Swallowing hard, Reyna watched as the man who claimed to be Davis Sinclair circled the front of the Jeep. The limp was much more noticeable this time, maybe because she was paying closer attention.

He yanked open her door and she shrank away from him. He lifted a brow at her reaction.

"Ready?" he said as he leaned in to give her a hand. Reyna's breath stuck in her throat, her heart drumming a mile a minute. She blamed it on the fact she'd been living in fear and the near-death experience—anything but the handsome, mysterious man by her side.

Their eyes met and her chest tightened. He was so close. She could see every line etched around his eyes, the deep grooves framing his full lips that spoke of someone who had chosen to live a life of solitude for a reason.

She had to get a grip. If this was indeed Jase Bradford, then she needed his help. But first she had to find out what he was hiding other than his true identity.

"Yes, I'm ready." Her voice sounded as if she'd run a marathon, and her hands shook. She sucked in her bottom lip, a nervous habit she couldn't break.

His attention shifted to her lips, his own breathing labored. She took his proffered hand and got out. After what felt like a lifetime of seconds ticking by in perfect cadence with her heart, he moved away and she was able to relax.

"Let's get you inside. Watch your step. The porch is slippery." Reyna slowly followed him. She kept the bag containing the storage locker key close. The contents of that locker might just be the one thing that would keep her alive if those thugs found her. Agent Martin's threats had solidified things in her mind. Eddie's death was no accident.

As they neared the house, motion-sensor lights flashed on, illuminating the front of the place. The man calling himself Davis Sinclair lived as if he was expecting danger to show up at his door any moment.

The house was three stories and enormous in stature. Made entirely of full round logs, it looked as if it could withstand quite a few Colorado winters. She noticed surveillance cameras positioned to capture every possible angle of the house. Massive amounts of firewood were stockpiled along both sides of the porch. The place looked like a compound and about as impenetrable as the White House.

A trickle of unease ran through her and she uttered a silent prayer asking for God's reassurance that she was doing the right thing. With everything she had gone through, she couldn't let down her guard for a second. She was at the mercy of a man with secrets and could be walking into a trap.

Her boots slipped on the porch and he reached out to steady her. His large, muscular arms circled her waist and drew her close. She could feel the warmth radiating from his body. Just for a second she stilled. She was so tired and he was so strong. If she inched in just a little bit, she could lean in to his strength.

Reyna pulled away and gave herself a mental shake. His arms dropped to his side. No matter how desperate she felt or how much she might want to trust him, her life was at stake. He unlocked the house and stepped inside, yet Reyna hesitated. She stood in the entrance, surrounded by darkness, the only light coming from a dying fire in the fireplace. She wouldn't go inside until she knew what she was facing in there.

He seemed to read all her uncertainties, because he flipped on the overhead light, illuminating the room. No one waited inside to take her into custody. There was nothing scary or out of the ordinary. Just the evidence of a house occupied by one person.

Reyna slowly stepped in and closed the door. He stopped by the fireplace but stood quietly watching her, as if trying to gauge her threat level. Neither one trusted the other just yet.

She glanced around. Reyna had to admit, the room itself was impressive. The ceiling vaulted up to what looked like at least fourteen feet above them. A massive stacked-stone fireplace was the showpiece of the room. Windows facing out toward the drive would enable him to see for miles. No one was coming up to the house unannounced. None of which eased her fears one little bit. Who was he expecting to come after *him*?

Reyna stole a glance his way. He was still sizing her up. The overhead antler chandelier bathed the room in soft light and she was able to get her first good look at the man she believed to be Jase Bradford. He was incredibly tall and powerfully built, his collar-length blond hair swept back from his face, and he sported a neatly trimmed beard slightly darker than his hair. He was rugged in an outdoorsy, mountain-man way and had the most intense midnight-blue eyes she'd ever seen.

"There are a couple of bedrooms upstairs. You can take your pick. Sheets are clean and there's a spare bath at the end of the hall. Towels are in the linen closet."

Reyna didn't budge. If he was really and truly the man she believed him to be, she needed answers as to why he'd lied to her. He might just have saved her life, but that didn't mean she trusted him.

"You asked me why I was out on the road tonight

and I told you, but what about you? You said yourself the weather was terrible. It had obviously been snowing for hours. Why risk running off the road as I did or get stranded out there alone?"

The corner of his mouth turned up in what passed for a smile. "I'm not the enemy here, Reyna." Chills sped up her spine at his gravelly tone.

She lifted her chin. "And that's not really an answer. Stop playing games with me. I know you're lying about who you are."

His body grew rigid in response, but he didn't say anything.

"When Eddie first told me he didn't believe you were dead, I thought maybe he was suffering from PTSD or something similar. He certainly showed all the classic symptoms. Still, the obvious reason not to believe was that both Eddie and I were at the memorial ceremony for you."

She stared straight at him. "During those last few days before Eddie returned to duty, he kept insisting you faked your death because someone was trying to wipe out all the original members of the Scorpion team. He told me if anything happened to him and someone came to the house asking questions I should find you. Then I come here and I find someone who looks similar to Jase Bradford, who has the same limp as Eddie's description of your injuries indicated, and suddenly I'm starting to believe that my husband was right all along."

She waited for him to deny it. He didn't, and her heart dropped to her stomach. A single muscle flexing in his jaw was his only reaction, a telltale sign that what she said made him uncomfortable.

After a handful of seconds ticked by. He turned away,

gathered a couple of pieces of wood stacked next to the fireplace and then tossed them angrily onto the fire.

It was then that she saw it. The last piece of the puzzle that confirmed the truth. He had a scorpion tattoo on the inside of his left wrist. Eddie possessed the same tattoo. He'd told her the entire team had them. It was sort of a rite of passage. There would be only one reason this man would have it. He was the leader of the CIA's Scorpion team.

Shivers racked through her, rendering her breathless. She was right. This *was* Jase Bradford.

Reyna looked as if she'd suffered a terrible shock. She had turned deathly pale and was staring at his wrist. She'd seen the tattoo. He regretted again his foolishness in keeping it.

While he tried to come up with a plausible denial, she dug into her pocket, pulled out a photo and held it out for him to see.

He never broke eye contact. "What's that?" he hedged.

"You tell me," she said, and shoved it closer into his line of sight.

He took it from her. It was a grainy photo taken a short time before the attack. He remembered the day they'd posed for it as if it was yesterday. His arm rested around Abby's waist. Eddie was standing next to Jase. Charlie, Brady and Steve Douglas in the background. The picture had been taken on Eddie's phone by the fifth member of their team. Their Afghanistan guide, Benjahah.

He stared at the phantoms in the photo. They had been invincible back then. They'd liberated a small village from a Taliban stronghold that day, each member of the team so full of life and promise. It was only Eddie's second mission with the team, yet already he'd become like one of the gang. Now they were all dead with the exception of him.

He glanced from the photo to Reyna. "Where did you get this?"

"I found it inside Eddie's laptop bag. It's true. Don't deny it. You are the person in that photo. You *are* Jase Bradford. I wasn't completely sure until I saw the tattoo." She grabbed his wrist and turned it up for them both to see.

He closed his eyes. Over the past three years, he'd thought about having it removed over a dozen times. But in the end, he'd kept the scorpion tattoo as a constant reminder of the woman he'd loved and the friends who had lost their lives instead of him.

"Eddie had one just like it. He told me everyone on the team got the same tattoo. It was like some sort of bond between you all. He was so excited to get his. So proud to join the elite Scorpions. So honored to work with you."

He couldn't move. Her words were like a knife to his heart. He didn't pull away, couldn't deny the truth.

Reyna let him go and went for the kill. "Why'd you lie to me and say you didn't know Jase Bradford after I told you I was Eddie's wife? You knew he was dead. I wouldn't be here without good reason. You saw how terrified I was and you lied to me. Answer me…*please*," she said desperately. "You owe me."

His breath hung in his throat as he gazed down at her. *You owe me…*

He'd been expecting his past to return for years. As such, he'd deliberately set the house up to be a virtual Fort Knox. Had weapons hidden everywhere on the property. Traps set. He'd gone over every possible attack scenario and figured out a means of escape. Still, *nothing* he had planned prepared him for the repercussions of facing Eddie's beautiful, grieving widow.

"At first…well, you looked different from the man in the photo. You're older. The beard and the hair threw me. When I saw the limp, it all started to add up. With the injuries you sustained that night, your leg would have been shattered, so naturally there would be a limp."

He tried to regain his cool, but it was next to impossible when he saw the condemnation flashing in her eyes. He didn't want to have this conversation with her. Didn't want to have to try to explain why he'd let Eddie down.

"My husband believed in you. He trusted you to help me." She huffed out an angry breath. "Well, obviously he was wrong. He believed in what you stood for back then…but look where it got him! You left him alone, and the people who took out your entire unit ended up killing him."

Killing him? She believed Eddie's death was not in the line of duty. If that were true, then had he and Kyle been wrong about it being the result of the failed weapons raid in Tora Bora?

Which meant…he had been wrong, too. Dead wrong. He thought Eddie was safe at Langley, but that clearly hadn't been the case. Now, the reality that he was responsible for his friend's death was almost too much to bear.

A dam broke inside of him. Emotions he thought he'd killed off long ago resurfaced and he squeezed his eyes shut.

"Yes, I'm Jase Bradford." His tone flatlined. He couldn't believe he had actually admitted the truth to another living soul. "At least, I used to be. I've tried to bury the man I was for so long, but he's still in here some-where." He held his fist to his chest.

Relief fought with shock as she watched him with-out so much as a word.

"And you're right… I do owe Eddie. There's not a day that goes by that I don't wish I'd never gotten him involved in the CIA." He smiled bitterly at her reaction. "Your husband was a good man. If he hadn't met me, he'd probably still be alive today, and for that I am truly sorry."

Jase regretted again his part in her pain.

"Reyna, I can see you're scared. I'm guessing you are being threatened because of something that hap-pened with Eddie. It doesn't matter." Holding her gaze, Jase tried to swallow back the lump in his throat, but it wouldn't go away. "Whatever reason brought you here, of course I'll help you. Eddie was my friend and I'd do anything for him."

"Thank you." She moved close, smiling up at him as if the weight of the world had been lifted, and then clutched his hand in gratitude.

"Why are you being followed, Reyna?" he asked.

She hitched in a breath and kept her answer brief. "Because I have something they want."

Before he could ask what she meant, a noise outside grabbed his full attention. A vehicle was coming up the mountain. He quickly extinguished the lights.

"What are you doing?" she asked.

"Someone's coming. Stay here." Jase grabbed his Glock from the mantel and the thermal-vision binoc-ulars he kept near the door and stepped out into the crisp night. The storm continued to dump snow and ice everywhere, but at least the wind had died down. He listened to the muffled quietness and then he heard it again. Off in the distance, probably five miles still down the mountain, more than one vehicle coming this way.

He scanned the mountainside with the binoculars and spotted movement on the ridge across the valley. His heart leaped in his throat. Had they stationed lookouts or—worse—snipers in case he and Reyna tried to escape before the extraction team arrived? If they had followed her all this way, she must have something extremely valuable to them. Why hadn't they taken her before now, under less dangerous conditions? Unless they were hoping she would lead them to him first.

Out of the corner of his eye, he caught sight of multiple flashes. Jase turned back to the door. The noise of rapid gunfire from an automatic weapon exploded around him. From inside Reyna screamed as a bullet whistled past his left ear. Before he could hit the ground, another grazed across his shoulder, the impact knocking him flat on his back. Blood oozed from the wound and coated his sleeve. A second round of shots took out the engine on the Jeep, along with the tires, rendering it useless.

His pulse kicked into overdrive as he struggled to make sense of it. Had he been wrong about Reyna? She'd seemed innocent enough, but what did he really know about her beyond the fact that she claimed to be Eddie's wife? Maybe she'd been sent here to find him by the same people who had taken out his entire team. Maybe Reyna Peterson was really just a cold-blooded killer.

THREE

Jase crawled on his hands and knees inside the house and slammed the door shut behind him.

"What happened out there?" She spotted the blood. "Jase, you're hurt. Did they shoot you?" Reyna's voice shook so much that he barely understood the words.

He leaped to his feet. "Not directly. The bullet grazed my shoulder. My guess is that was deliberate. If they'd been trying to seriously injure me they would have. It's just a flesh wound."

He needed answers. "You said you have something they want. Tell me who they are, Reyna. Who's following you?"

Wide-eyed, she stared at him. "I don't know…"

His patience slipped closer to the breaking point. "Don't give me that. You know something. Why else did you come all this way to find a dead man?"

"I don't know who they are, okay?" she retorted. "But I think they're the same men who came to my house and threatened me."

He looked at her in shock. "They threatened you? Why?"

"I don't know. They came to my house and accused Eddie of being a traitor. They said he'd…taken something and if I didn't give it back I could end up in a federal prison or worse." She exhaled shakily. "Jase, I think these men are responsible for killing Eddie. And now they're coming after us. We need to get out of here."

It took him a second to process what she'd said. "You think Eddie was murdered. That doesn't make any sense. Unless you have proof that someone wanted him dead?"

She looked away. "Not exactly."

"What does 'not exactly' mean?" The noise of approaching vehicles grew louder. As much as he needed to know more about the danger she'd brought to his door, it would have to wait.

He blew out a blustery sigh. "We need to leave now. There are multiple vehicles heading our way."

"Let me take a look at your shoulder first."

"There's no time," he said in a hard tone. He added quietly, "It can wait. I'll be fine." He grabbed a couple of thick wool jackets from the hall closet and stuffed a small towel inside his shirt to absorb the blood.

Jase handed her one of the jackets. "Here, put this on. It'll help in keeping them from tracking you through thermal imagery. Wool helps to conceal body heat."

She slipped into the oversize jacket. "They must have followed me somehow." She unknowingly confirmed what he suspected. "But I was so careful."

"Did you tell anyone you were coming here?" She'd seemed so innocent with her story of Eddie, but what if she was just a tool to get to him all along?

"No…and I did everything I could to make sure I wasn't being tailed."

"They found you some way." His eyes flicked to her face.

"No one knows I'm here, Jase," she assured him. "I did call my friend Sara once I arrived in Defiance to let her know I was okay… That's her car down the mountain, which I borrowed because I was worried they'd find a way to track mine. I trust Sara completely. She's my best friend. I never would have made it through Eddie's death without her. But I never told anyone— her included—where I was going." He was impressed. She'd put some thought into her getaway.

It might be the worst mistake of his life, but Jase believed her. "Give me your phone."

She made no move to do so. "Why?"

"They had to track you somehow, Reyna. I'm guessing it may have been through your phone call."

"That's not possible. No one has the number…"

"Except for your friend," he pointed out. "Maybe they traced the call you made to her. Either way, we need to get rid of it."

She dug into her tote bag and handed him the phone. Jase didn't hesitate. He tossed it into the fire, grabbed her arm and headed for the back of the house. "We have to get out of here now. They'll be here soon."

"Where are you going? Why aren't we taking the Jeep?"

"It's destroyed. They took it out to keep us from getting away." He tossed his answer over his shoulder without looking at her. "Thankfully, they have no way of knowing I have another vehicle stashed down the mountain."

She followed him to the back door and waited while he donned the second jacket. "Here, hold on to me. We can't risk using the flashlight. Do your best to stay as quiet as you can. Noise carries for miles up here."

She clasped the hand he held out to her. The tremors in hers betrayed her fear and Jase's heart went out to her. He would do whatever it took to protect Eddie's widow or he'd die trying.

He stepped off the back deck and she followed. "We'll have to take it slow. There's some pretty rough terrain back here," his whispered against her ear. "Just stay close and don't let go of my hand. It's going to be okay."

They headed past the storage shed at the back of the house and slowly down the mountain. They'd covered a quarter of a mile before he stopped to listen for a second. He couldn't hear the noise of the engines anymore. The men had reached the house. It wouldn't take them long to realize he and Reyna had escaped out the back.

Jase flinched as he tested his shoulder. It hurt like crazy, making him aware of every little move he made. Reyna saw his pain and she came closer and unbuttoned his jacket and shirt. He tensed as she examined the wound with gentle fingers. She took the towel, snugged it as tight as she could to stem the bleeding, then closed his shirt and jacket back up. "It should be okay until we reach the vehicle."

"Thanks," he gritted out. "We have to hurry. They're at the house. It won't be long before they come after us. It's not much farther to the Land Cruiser."

Reyna nodded, but he could see she was exhausted already. She'd been through enough to send most people to the breaking point and this night wasn't close to being over.

They continued their treacherous trek through the woods, but finding the stashed vehicle in the dark in the middle of a snowstorm was next to impossible. He'd deliberately hid it well. It took him a few minutes to gain his bearings and then he whispered a prayer of gratitude when he finally spotted it.

"This way." He pointed at the dark shape to his left. He glanced behind them and saw a half dozen flashlights fanning out behind his house.

"They're coming. Hurry, Reyna." She looked over her shoulder and saw what he did.

He let go of her hand and she followed him over to the camouflaged tarp covering the vehicle. Jase went about removing the tarp as quickly as possible.

One of the men with flashlights yelled to his comrades, "Hey, back here. I see them. They have another vehicle. They're getting away!"

"Hop in and buckle up. It's going to be a rough trip downhill," Jase told her, and waited while Reyna braced one foot against the running board and boosted herself inside.

He rushed to the driver's side. Behind them, he could hear engines firing once more. He started the SUV and shoved it into Drive.

Reyna reached for the grab handle above her door and braced herself against the jarring ride. She glanced back behind them. "Jase, they're still coming," she said in a tense tone.

He tried to reassure her. "We'll be okay. We have the advantage. I know the layout of the land. They don't. Hang on!"

The Land Cruiser bounced along the rough terrain lurching over brush and dead tree parts. Jase clenched his jaw to keep from grunting in pain. He checked the rearview mirror and could see five sets of headlights.

"So far, they're not gaining on us. No doubt they're taking it slow until they get familiar with the landscape." He glanced her way. "That won't take long. They appear to be highly trained. Probably former military."

"They're not going to give up. They'll keep coming

until they have what they want," she said desperately. "We can't let that happen."

"I'm not going to let those thugs hurt you, Reyna."

She stared at him for a moment, then slowly nodded. She believed him.

Jase had a white-knuckle grip on the steering wheel, his shoulder wound throbbing every inch of the way. He jerked the wheel in time to dodge a stump only to be launched into midair by a rock he'd completely forgotten.

The SUV shot the rest of the way off the mountain and onto a gravel road. Jase killed the lights and floored the gas pedal. They needed to put as much distance as they could if his plan was going to work.

"Hang tight, I have an idea. This road leads to a small town called Glazer. We're going to head that way and then go off-road and circle back. If I'm good at concealing our tracks, I'm hoping those men will think we continued on to Glazer."

"Don't you need the lights to see? It's pitch-black out." Reyna shot him worried look.

"We can't afford to use them," he said, keeping his focus on the darkness in front of them. "They'll see the lights and follow us."

He drove another five or six miles down the gravel road to Glazer all the while checking the rearview mirror. So far, nothing.

Jase slowed to a stop when he saw thick brush growing near the edge of the road. "Here. This is our best place to leave the road." Jase edged the Land Cruiser from the road, drove into the wooded area some ways up and stopped. He turned to her. "I'm going to do my best to conceal what little tracks we might have left behind. Stay here."

Jase waited for her to say something. When she didn't, he squeezed her hand. "I'll be right back."

He jogged back down the path they'd just traversed. Other than a few squashed bushes there was no discernible evidence the Land Cruiser had left the road. On this side of the mountain the trees hung close to the road sheltering it from the brunt of the storm.

Jase did his best to straighten the bushes and then hurried back to the Land Cruiser.

He put the vehicle in gear. "There's a small logging road a little ways from here. It's not used much anymore, so it's not on any map and no one but the locals know about it. It should bring us out on the other side of Defiance."

It had been a while since he'd been four-wheeling this way and the landscape had changed quite a bit. It took several minutes to spot the logging road down below.

Jase eased the Land Cruiser onto it. "Hopefully they bought the diversion. It so, it will take our friends a little while to realize we gave them the slip. That will buy us some much-needed time."

It took all his skills to maneuver the Land Cruiser down the road without the headlights. After what felt like a lifetime, Jase saw the lights of Defiance.

He hit the brakes and the vehicle slid on the ice some fifteen feet and then spun toward the ditch before it finally came to a grinding stop.

"Thank You, Lord." He breathed the prayer aloud, then turned to Reyna. She had her eyes closed, her hands braced on the dash. "Are you okay?"

Slowly she opened her eyes and nodded. "Yes, I think so. How about you? How's the shoulder?"

He could feel beads of sweat on his forehead. "It's holding up all right, but I think it's time for that bandage. There's a first-aid kit in the back. I'll get it and be right back."

He hopped out of the SUV and walked a little ways behind it. Listening carefully, he heard the noise of engines fading into the distance. The men chasing them were continuing on the road to Glazer. They had time to breathe, but it wouldn't last long. He and Reyna needed to make good of the advantage they'd been given, which meant he had to find out what she had that those men wanted.

What troubled him the most was Reyna's conviction that Eddie had been murdered. It just didn't add up in his mind. What could Eddie have possibly gotten involved in to end his life?

Jase drew in a deep breath and fell back on the training he'd received from one of the best in the spy business. The man who had taught him how to survive when his back was against the wall and there was nowhere to turn. Kyle Jennings had been a legend by the time Jase signed on. He'd recruited Jase straight out of the university and had become his handler as Jase had moved up through the ranks to lead the Scorpion team.

Jase could almost hear Kyle reprimanding him now. *Go back to the cause of the matter. Start there. Figure out why our men had to die.*

He remembered the key he'd found in Reyna's bag. Obviously, it fit something important, because she hadn't let the bag out of her sight for a minute. He needed to find out what it belonged to.

Realizing he was wasting valuable time, Jase dug out his first-aid kit and got back in the Land Cruiser.

"They aren't following us. We're safe for now."

Reyna blew out a visible sigh of relief. "Good. Honestly, I can't believe all of the things that have happened recently."

When he didn't answer, she took the first-aid kit from him, rifled through it and began to examine his wound. Her full attention on the job at hand, he studied her while she was unaware of him. Her lustrous brown hair, much the worse for wear after their grueling hike, hung loose around her shoulders. She'd lost her ponytail holder somewhere along the way and he doubted she were even conscious of it. Swallowing convulsively, he resisted the urge to brush away a silky strand that had fallen in her face. He was letting his chaotic emotions get the better of him.

Reyna tore the rest of his shirt away from his arm and he froze. He wasn't used to people taking care of him. Her eyes locked with his. Hers were huge pools of green. She drew in a breath and he realized he was staring at her full lips, thinking things that couldn't fit into his life.

"Let me take care of your wound properly," she managed in a soft, soothing voice.

Jase tried to gather his straying thoughts. "There's no time. We have to keep moving. They could have snipers on this side of the mountain. A roadblock." The possibilities were limitless.

She didn't listen. Instead, she dabbed the wound thoroughly while he tried not to wince as the antiseptic hit the exposed area, and then she stuck a bandage over it.

"There. That should keep it from being infected. I can do a more thorough job once we're…safe," she added as an afterthought, then moved away.

He prayed that moment would come.

"Jase, we could have died back there." Her words

tumbled out, but he could barely hear what she said over his own pounding heart. His reaction to her was completely unexpected. "What do we do now?"

"I'd say that depends on you."

Her delicate brow knit in confusion. "I don't understand."

"I think you do. No more secrets, Reyna. As you can see, these thugs are deadly serious. You said yourself you believe they murdered Eddie for something you have. Tell me what they're willing to kill for."

Throughout the frantic drive to Defiance, Reyna had asked God for guidance. Prayed for proof Eddie hadn't been delusional. Then she'd discovered Jase was really alive, as her husband had believed, and now in the space of a few hours he'd risked his life to save hers…twice. But could she trust him? She turned in her seat so that she could see him more clearly.

"Why did you come here to me, Reyna?" he asked, his indigo-blue eyes piercing into hers. "Who are those people following you? If you want me to keep you safe, you're going to have to tell me what's really going on."

His questions hit a little too close to home and an unfamiliar battle raged inside her. She was normally a straightforward person, but she couldn't get past the fact that Jase Bradford was harboring secrets of his own.

Reyna decided to lay it all on the line. "I do need your help, but I'm sorry, I don't trust you. You lied to me."

She could see from the muscle ticking in his jaw that her declaration stung.

"You're right… I did, but only out of self-preservation. I didn't fake my death without a good cause, Reyna. Somebody wanted me dead. They still do. I had to be certain you weren't working for those people."

"And are you?" she asked curiously.

"I hope so," he answered after a moment.

Not exactly the answer she wanted to hear, but at least she now knew where they stood. They were two people forced to trust each other when their lives depended on it.

"So now you understand how I felt when you lied to me. *You* could be part of *them*."

"Them?" he snatched at the word. "Who are you talking about?"

"I'll do my best to explain, but it's so hard. I feel as if I'm drowning in what-ifs," she said with frustration. "This is so far beyond my understanding. Nothing about it makes sense."

His expression softened as he watched her. "I get that. Tell me what happened to Eddie. Why do you think he was murdered? How is his death connected to the people following you?"

Taking a deep breath, Reyna struggled to let go of her misgivings about Jase. "I should start by telling you Eddie left the CIA a year after your…death."

Her revelation clearly floored him. "You're kidding." She watched the color seep from his ruggedly handsome face. "Why would he leave the Agency? He loved the job and he was working in Langley. He was safe."

She stared at him, surprised. "What do you mean he was safe?"

Something came and went in Jase's expression before she could name it. He cleared his throat. "Only that he wasn't in a war zone. Did he tell you why he left the CIA?"

She couldn't dispel the feeling that Jase hadn't told her everything. He kept his secrets close. Eddie had, as well, and look where they'd gotten him. It seemed to be part of the job description when you were a spy. "He never really said. He just came home one day and told me he was done with it. And that he'd joined the Marines. I was speechless."

"The *Marines*?" Jase looked baffled. "What happened to him? How was he killed?"

Reyna would never forget that day. It was imprinted into her memory like an indelible stamp. "Two men showed up at my door and told me Eddie was dead. One was a marine. The second man was dressed in a suit. He never identified himself. The marine told me Eddie's platoon had been hit by sniper fire. The strange thing is, Eddie was the only one who died. No one else sustained injuries. It seemed almost as if he was the only target."

Jase never broke eye contact. "You're right, it does sound peculiar." He thought for a second and then asked, "Was the second guy CIA?"

"That was my guess, but he never said, and I don't understand why the CIA would show up. Eddie wasn't with the Agency at the time of his death. Anyway, it had me curious so I called Kyle Jennings and left a message. I never heard back from him." She studied Jase. Something about what she said obviously made him uneasy.

More secrets.

If it weren't for the urgent call she'd received from Eddie shortly before he died, she might not have thought anything about his death was out of the ordinary. But Eddie's call had shaken her.

She shared the details of the conversation with Jase. "My husband was scared for his life. He kept repeating 'I wasn't able to prove what happened. Tell him I'm sorry I wasn't able to prove what happened.' I had no idea what he was talking about."

But Jase clearly did. He looked as if he'd been punched in the gut.

"What is it?" she asked.

He looked away. "Nothing. Go on."

She sighed and stared out at the darkness. "They didn't want me to view his body, but I insisted. I had to see him one last time." She shook her head. "It was… the hardest thing I've ever done. I barely recognized him. They told me his injuries were severe."

"I'm so sorry," Jase said gently. "That must have been so difficult."

She drew in a quavering breath. "It was…heart-breaking, seeing him like that."

Reyna watched as Jase glanced into the rearview mirror once more. She looked over her shoulder. "You think they'll keep coming after us."

"Without a doubt. Which is why we need to get off this road as quickly as possible. It's best if we keep moving for the time being." He peered through the wind-shield at the sky. A handful of stars had popped out. "The storm's letting up at least."

Jase put the Land Cruiser in gear. "You still haven't told me what you have that those men want." He spared her a glance.

The gravel road dead-ended onto pavement that appeared to be at the opposite end of town from where Reyna had entered. Nothing looked familiar. The compass in the console said they were heading due north. Just the opposite direction of where she had stashed the laptop. She wasn't going to leave without it. Whatever was on it had been significant enough for Eddie to risk his life to get it out of a war zone. The laptop was her only bargaining chip. Which meant, like it or not, she had to tell Jase where she'd left it. "I have a laptop that

Eddie hid before he died. We have to go back for it."
Reyna briefly explained about the letter she'd received
from Eddie.

Jase brought the SUV to an abrupt stop on the shoulder of the road and faced her. She could see she had his
full attention.

He ran a hand across his stubbled jaw. "I can't even
imagine how difficult it must have been receiving a letter from Eddie after his death."

"It was…so horrible. Almost like losing him all over
again, and the note was extremely cryptic. He started
out by saying how much he loved me and looked forward to us being together soon." Reyna's voice caught
and she blinked back tears. "Then he mentioned our
first date."

She thought the letter was frightening until the men
had shown up at her door and threatened her. "I didn't
understand what he was trying to tell me until I thought
about where Eddie took me for our first date. You see,
Eddie's family owns a farm outside of Stevens, Texas."

Reyna remembered how emotionally difficult it was
to go back to the farm.

She drew in a breath. "We went on a picnic there for
our first date and afterward we went horseback riding.
So I went back to the farm and I found the laptop in a
fireproof box in the stable where they used to keep the
horses. Eddie hid it there along with the photo of the
Scorpions. I realize now that since you and I had never
met, he wanted me to know what you looked like." She
paused for a long moment. "My guess is he hid it the last
time he came home on leave. I remember he was acting
strangely. He was paranoid someone was watching him.
He'd disappear for long periods of time."

"He knew you'd be the only one who would know

where to find it," Jase said. "Sounds like Eddie went to a lot of trouble to keep it from falling into the wrong hands. What's on it?"

"I wish I knew." She sighed impatiently. "Jase, there are a bunch of photos that I don't understand and another file that's encrypted."

He continued to watch her as if trying to ascertain whether she was telling the truth. "Where is it? We can't go to the car. They'll have found it by now."

"It's not in the car. I thought if they caught up with me, they'd search the car and find it. Then they wouldn't need me anymore. I couldn't take the risk."

"You left it in a storage facility somewhere," he concluded.

She looked surprised. "Yes. How did you know?"

"I found the key in your bag."

The key. He knew about the key, which meant he'd gone through her things. "You had no right going through my stuff!"

"I think I've earned the right."

Anger flashing in her eyes, she clamped her mouth shut.

Jase blew out an annoyed breath. "Look, Reyna, whoever's following you won't go away until they have the laptop. Something on it is of vital importance to them, which means not only do they need the laptop but they will want to silence you once they have it. They can't afford to leave any witnesses behind." He leaned in closer, his warm breath fanning against her skin. "After what just happened, I'd think that would be clear. If you want my help, tell me where it is."

She hesitated then said, "There's a small town southwest of here. Eldorado. It's there."

Reyna watched him process this new bit of information. "I've been there before. Eldorado is a good seven-hour drive from here."

She tried to determine what he was thinking but couldn't. "I'm not leaving Colorado without it. You said yourself what's on it is extremely valuable to these men. It is to me, also. Please, Jase. I can't do this without you. I need your help."

He watched her for a long moment before responding. "Okay, let's go to Eldorado." Jase put the SUV in gear and did a U-turn in the middle of the road.

As they headed southwest, Reyna settled back in her seat and closed her eyes, pretending to rest. She wished she trusted the man seated next to her the way Eddie obviously had, but if the past few days had taught her anything, it was that nothing and nobody were as they seemed. Especially a former spy.

FOUR

"*Babe, if anything happens to me don't let them get away with it.*"

"*What's going to happen to you? Eddie, what are you afraid of?*"

Her husband tried to laugh away her concerns, but his laughter didn't quite reach his eyes. "Nothing. Forget I said anything. I'm just being paranoid."

On impulse, she added, "Eddie, don't go back. Stay here with me. I'm sure we can get you out of your commitment. We can call Kyle. He'll be able to help. Please, don't go back there."

"No. Kyle can't help. I have to go, babe. It's my turn," he told her simply.

"Your turn? Your turn for what?"

He leaned over and kissed her sweetly. "It's my turn to die."

"Eddie..." She reached out to touch him, but he disappeared before her eyes.

"No! Eddie, no!" Reyna cried out, and then an instant before she could hold him one last time, she awoke.

She was crying. It was just a dream. She'd had that same one dozens of times since Eddie's death, reliving those final words he spoke to her before he left for

Afghanistan. Each time after she awakened, she was no closer to finding the answers she was desperate for than when they had first told her about Eddie's demise.

Reyna struggled to shake off the dream's heartbreaking effects. She realized she was alone in the SUV. Jase was nowhere in sight. It was just getting light out and they were in Eldorado parked just down from a rundown café.

Where was he? Her heart slammed in her chest. Had he deliberately gone along with her plan to retrieve the laptop, and once he had it, he'd turn her over to the people following her? She'd been foolish to trust him.

Her panic became paralyzing. She frantically searched through her bag and found the key where she'd left it. Still, he could have convinced the storage clerk that he'd lost his key.

She had to get away before it was too late. Reyna grabbed the tote bag and quickly got out of the Land Cruiser. She started running toward the diner. She had no idea what she was doing.

She reached for the door when it opened and Jase emerged, carrying a bag and a couple of coffees.

He stopped dead midstride when he saw her. "Are you okay?" he asked in concern when he spotted the tote bag.

He'd gone for coffee. Relief made her limbs weak. He'd driven straight through the night. No doubt, he was exhausted and needed the caffeine.

"I just wanted to get some air," she said in a wobbly voice.

Jase pointed toward a couple of tables near the diner. "Do you want to sit for a bit? It's nice out and there's no one around right now." He glanced down at his watch.

"It's still early, and, according to the waitress, the storage facility doesn't open for another half hour."

Reyna forced a smile. "Yes, that would be nice. Thanks."

He took the tote from her and pulled out one of the chairs. "I've got cinnamon rolls and coffee. I hope you drink it, otherwise…"

Reyna was touched at the somewhat awkward yet chivalrous way he treated her. She had gotten the impression that he spent a lot of time alone—he clearly wasn't used to having people around. At any other time, she might have found his behavior charming.

"Thank you. Coffee's perfect."

He handed her a cup and opened the pastry bag. When he unwrapped a couple of cinnamon rolls, her stomach growled, reminding her of the length of time that had passed since she'd eaten.

"They look delicious," she said.

He grinned at her. "Help yourself. There's plenty."

Reyna took one of the cinnamon rolls and dumped sugar and cream into her coffee. With the coffee stirred to perfection, she took a bite of her cinnamon roll and closed her eyes.

"That good, huh?" He chuckled at her ecstatic expression.

"They're wonderful. Of course, part of it could be that I really don't remember the last time I ate anything."

Jase pulled his coffee close and took a sip without answering. She noticed he'd changed out of his bloody clothes.

He spotted her staring at his shirt. "I keep a change of clothing and some emergency supplies in the back of the Land Cruiser. In the mountains you never know when you're going to get caught out in bad weather."

She nodded. "How's your shoulder?" She could tell he favored it.

He grimaced. "A bit better. I switched out the bandage. It's stopped bleeding…just hurts like crazy. But I've had worse on a good day in Afghanistan."

She accepted his attempt to make light of his injury. Eddie had been the same way. Always the protector, never wanting to ask for help. It came with the territory. She couldn't imagine the horrible things they had witnessed.

She glanced around at the picturesque view before her. "You know, Eddie and I always talked about seeing the mountains one day…" A whimsical smile crossed her face.

"Really? Where did you guys want to go?"

"All over really. Eddie wanted to come to Colorado." Her expression sobered. "I wished he could have seen this. He would have loved it here. Minus the drama, of course." Tears were close and she struggled to hold them back. "It's hard going on with your life without the person you love. It's so unfair."

Jase nodded. "Yes." Something akin to grief came and went. She remembered Eddie telling her once about Jase and Abby's romance. She couldn't imagine the pain he'd gone through. Losing the woman he loved while having to go into hiding himself.

Reyna tentatively touched his hand. "Eddie mentioned that you and Abby were a couple."

He grew tense. A muscle worked in his jaw and he didn't answer.

"What was she like?" Reyna prompted because she

realized she wanted to know about the woman he'd once loved.

For the longest time, she wondered if he would answer. He stared at the table, looking into the past. "She was…beautiful and strong and she could hold her own against any obstacle thrown her way. I think I fell in love with her the moment I met her." A hint of a smile played at the corners of his mouth. "I still can't believe she's gone," he murmured. "The worst part was I never got to say goodbye."

"I'm so sorry."

"Thanks," he said, and cleared his throat and changed the subject. "Can you think of anything you may have forgotten to mention yet? I've been mulling over what you told me in my head and nothing adds up. It would help to know what we are up against."

She liked the way he used the word *we*. It made her feel as if she wasn't in this alone anymore. She thought about everything that had happened since Eddie's death. One thing in particular stood out. "There is something, but I'm not sure how it fits with anything. Shortly after Eddie died and I moved back to Stevens, Texas, someone new showed up at my church. A man. Former marine, he said, and he looked the part. The weird thing was it was as if he went out of his way to be my friend." She released a breath. "At first, I didn't think much of it. He seemed nice enough. Told me his name was Frank. He was pleasant to talk to until he mentioned something that caught my attention and sent my radar up."

"What was it?"

She hesitated, and he reached for her hands and clasped them together in his. "Please, let me help you."

The feel of his fingers entwined with hers sent an infusion of warmth flowing through her. She slowly nodded. She so desperately needed his help. "We were exchanging stories about the war. I told him some things Eddie mentioned to me and then he said something about the battle that resulted in your...disappearance, almost as if he'd been there himself, but that's impossible, because Eddie told me there hadn't been any military backup..." She stopped and looked at him.

Reyna could see this troubled him. "How did a former marine know about a failed secret CIA mission? Unless he was on a fishing expedition for someone. Did you ever see him again?"

She shook her head. "No. Something about his aggressive behavior sent up warning signals. I stopped going to my church because of him. He called a couple of times after that, but I didn't answer. I don't know how he got my number..." She stopped. "I guess that's a really silly question. He probably had it on file somewhere."

"I'm sure," he said, glancing up at a group of people passing by.

"There's more," she added suddenly.

"Like what?"

"To start with, right before Eddie died I received a package in the mail. There was no return address. When I opened it, I found the watch Eddie's grandfather gave him when he graduated high school. There was a note inside that read, 'Take care of it for me.' Jase, Eddie *never* took that watch off. Needless to say, that scared me, so I tried to reach Eddie but couldn't."

"Maybe he just wanted to keep it safe," Jase reasoned. "A war zone can be pretty violent."

"That's what I thought until I found out Eddie was killed a few days later. Then there's the fact that it took more than three months for the military to release Eddie's belongings." She recalled the callous way they'd delivered her husband's possessions. "I came home from work one evening and there was a box sitting on my porch with Eddie's name on it. It took over two and a half months before I could bring myself to open it without falling apart. When I finally did, lots of things were missing."

"Such as?" he pressed.

"Eddie's phone. His tablet. Some personal items. There was a picture of us taken while we were on our honeymoon at Virginia Beach. Eddie kept it with him always. Even his wedding ring was missing, along with some letters I wrote to him shortly before he died." She paused for a moment. "There were only a few articles of clothing, his tags inside. But that's not the scary part. Shortly after I reported Eddie's missing belongings to the military, those men showed up at my doorstep late one night."

"That's when you left your home?"

"Yes, that very night. They scared me to death, Jase." Her lower lip trembled and she bit down on it. She'd seen some pretty frightening things as a doctor, but what had happened to her that night kept her awake at night. "I was terrified I'd lose my freedom if not my life."

Jase squeezed her fingers. "I can imagine." The strength she felt in his callused hands helped her continue.

"They told me if I didn't produce the laptop soon they'd be back and have me arrested for treason and I'd never see the light of day again—or worse."

Anger flared in his eyes. "That was a bluff. They have no authority over you. They were trying to frighten you."

"Well, it worked. I knew I had to leave. I borrowed Sara's car, found the laptop and headed for Colorado."

Suddenly wary, Jase looked at the growing number of people milling around. Tourists were pouring into the town and it was becoming harder to determine who might be a possible threat. In the short time they'd been talking it had started to snow again.

"We need to go. This place is getting crowded. Let's get the laptop and get out of here while we still can."

Jase stopped in front of a store window and pretended to glance at the items on display while carefully studying the people passing by. He was trying to make sure they hadn't been followed from the café. To call less attention to themselves they'd decided to walk the short distance to the storage facility.

So far, no one around them set off his internal radar.

He glanced at his watch. "The place should be open by now."

Over the noise of the crowd, it was impossible to hear much. They turned the corner onto another street and he was happy to see there were fewer people.

"How did you and Eddie meet anyway?" Jase asked, mostly to keep her mind off the possible danger they faced. Eddie had once told him they'd met very young.

Reyna didn't seem to mind the distraction. "I was in first grade and Eddie was one grade ahead of me. My family had just moved to Stevens. I was the new kid in school and I was incredibly shy. Eddie took me under his wing and showed me the ropes. We became inseparable from that moment on. We were in junior high when he told me he was going to marry me."

"And he did." He smiled down at her.

"Yes, he did." Something dark and turbulent entered

her eyes. "Back then he was so carefree. He loved life so much, but in those last few months before he died, Eddie changed drastically. I barely recognized him."

"How so?"

"When he came home on leave before the final mission…he'd lost weight. He wasn't sleeping. He was restless." She sighed wearily. "Whenever we'd go out anywhere, he was constantly checking the rearview mirror as if he thought someone was following us, and when we were home, he'd make at least a dozen trips to the living room window, looking for…something. He was petrified, Jase."

None of the behavior Reyna mentioned sounded like the upbeat man Jase remembered. "Did he say what he was so afraid of?"

"No, and I begged him to tell me what was going on, but he said he couldn't. It was best I didn't know. He spent hours in the garage. I asked what he was doing but he wouldn't say." She glanced up at Jase. "And he talked in his sleep a lot. He had terrible nightmares where he kept repeating someone was killing off the original members of the Scorpion team. He said it wasn't what it seemed. Do you have any idea what he meant?"

His expression froze in place. If only he could answer that question. He glanced ahead of them, but really he was right back in the war zone reliving those last few fateful missions as he had so many times before. Searching for answers just out of his grasp.

"You do know what he meant. What happened, Jase?" she pressed. She'd seen something in him. He'd given it away. One incident in particular stood out in his mind. It still haunted him. Like it or not, Reyna was just as embroiled in this as he was. She had the right to know everything.

"We were deep in enemy territory, searching for stolen weapons," he said in a barely audible voice. "This was sometime before Eddie joined the team. We'd set out on foot. The team spread out in groups. We had drone footage confirming the weapons were in a warehouse less than eighteen hours earlier." He took a breath, let it out slowly.

"Abby and I circled to the back side. Benjahah, our Afghan guide, was with us. When we raided the place, we took fire." He scraped a hand across his face. "Benjahah...he simply disappeared. I thought maybe he was hit because he was there one minute and then...he wasn't. We ended up capturing five insurgents. A handful escaped. The scary part was the weapons that had been there a short time earlier had disappeared into thin air."

She stared at him wide eyed. "Where did they go?"

"My guess is someone knew we were coming. They made sure the weapons disappeared. We were wrapping up the mission when I spotted Benjahah coming out of the woods. The same direction as some of the men who escaped had gone. He was out of breath and looked guilty as all get-out."

"Did you confront him?"

"I did." Jase's mouth twisted bitterly. "He said he'd become surrounded by the enemy and he couldn't escape so he hid because he was scared they'd capture and interrogate him. In the past, Benjahah was fearless. I could tell he was lying."

"Unbelievable," Reyna huffed.

"Yes. I started thinking back to before that mission and I remembered how many times Benjahah had simply disappeared for a few hours while we were inactive. He said he was visiting friends, but I think he was meeting with his terrorist contact." He shook his head. "Anyway, it wasn't too long after the incident that members of our team began to die. First, it was Thomas and Mason. Both were killed during a failed weapons mission." Back then, Jase had still believed their deaths had been in the line of duty.

Losing two agents so suddenly had left a hole in the unit. Jase had recruited Eddie to fill the void.

"After Thomas and Mason died Eddie joined the team. Soon after, Benjahah left the team. He said he wanted a change. I found out later that he died in an enemy attack outside of Beirut."

Reyna gaped at him in amazement. "Do you think he was part of what happened to the team? Why would they kill him if he was helping them?"

"Maybe he became too much of a liability so he had to be silenced."

Reyna shook her head. "So you think Eddie was right. Someone was systematically taking out members of the original Scorpions."

He cleared his throat. "I believe so. After that final attack that killed so many of our team and shattered my leg, I was airlifted to a military hospital stateside. Kyle met me there and told me my days were numbered. The people responsible for taking out most of the team hadn't been successful in killing me abroad, but they weren't going to stop until they completed their mission." His face blanched as he forced the words out.

"I remember how shocked Eddie was to learn about your death," Reyna told him. "He was so certain you would recover. When we found out you'd died from your injuries, he took the news very hard."

Jase tried to read Reyna's reaction but couldn't. Did she think him a coward? "Kyle came up with the plan to fake my death. If it hadn't been for him getting me out of the hospital when he did, I believe I'd be dead now."

He saw the shock in her eyes. "It's true, Reyna. The day before I…disappeared, someone came into my room pretending to be a doctor. I was in bad shape and in and out of consciousness. Kyle just happened to stop by. He'd been keeping a close eye on me. The man claimed he was there to administer a new medication."

Jase could see he had Reyna's full attention.

"Kyle suspected the man was lying. The more he questioned him, the cagier he became. Kyle attempted to take him into custody, but the man went crazy. He shoved a food tray cart in front of Kyle and managed to escape." Jase raked a hand through his hair. "That made it real for me. One way or another, Jase Bradford had to cease to exist. Kyle had a friend, a doctor who worked at the same hospital. He signed my death certificate. Kyle made the official announcement and then he smuggled me out of the hospital one night and took me to a cabin in Montana for rehab. Later he arranged the memorial service."

"Oh, Jase." Reyna reached out and gently cupped his jaw. "That must have been horrible. I can't imagine what you went through."

It was horrible. Still today, the thought of how difficult that trip had been, traveling thousands of miles when he was so severely injured. Well, he knew God had been there with him every step of the way.

He covered her hand with his. "It was the hardest thing I've ever done. We ended up holed up at a run-down motel for a couple of weeks until I was able to make the hike down to the cabin. I stayed at the cabin there almost two months healing…physically."

That time stood out in his mind as dark and dismal. "I never would have made it without Kyle."

Reyna looked up at him, her face softening with empathy. "I know exactly what you mean. After Eddie died, I couldn't stand being in DC any longer so I moved back home to Texas. I bought a house in a quiet neighborhood, yet even with the change, I couldn't move on. It was as if I were simply marking time. I felt so alone." Her lips trembled ever so slightly as she spoke. "Then, a few weeks after I moved in, Sara came over and introduced herself. She was new to the neighborhood, too. We became good friends. It was as if God sent her into my life. We helped each other grieve. Her husband had died in a car accident some years before so we had a lot in common."

Reyna and Jase started walking again. Up ahead, Jase spotted the storage facility and tugged Reyna into the entryway of a vacant store. "I think I should go in alone just in case. They'll be looking for you. There's still the chance they don't know I'm alive, and even if they do, you said yourself my appearance has changed," he added when she hesitated.

It hurt to see the distrust in her eyes, yet he understood. She'd been through so much. Her reluctance to let go of the one piece of the puzzle keeping her safe was human, but he needed to find out what was in those files if he was going to help her.

"I promise I'm on your side." He tried to reassure her. "I know it's hard but you have to trust me."

She stared into his eyes for the longest time, searching for reassurance. Finally, she must have found it because Reyna dug into the bag and retrieved the key. "It's number sixteen." She handed it to him.

"Thank you. Stay here. If I'm not back in ten minutes, or if you spot anything out of the ordinary, duck inside one of these tourist shops and slip out the back door." He took out the Land Cruiser keys and handed them to her along with his phone. "Go back to the Land Cruiser and get out of town. Don't wait for me. I'll find you."

"I'm not leaving you here."

Her concern for him wasn't earned and it humbled him. He silently prayed to one day be worthy of it. "Reyna, I can't let anything to happen to you. I *won't*. Don't worry about me. Just promise me." He gripped her arms and held her gaze. "Please, I have to know that you're safe."

"Okay," she said a little breathlessly.

Swallowing hard, Jase reached down and framed her face in his hands. She was so beautiful and she looked so worried he'd give just about anything to ease it away for her. As he continued to gaze down at her, his pulse pounding in his ears, he realized the desire to protect her went far deeper than loyalty to his friend.

"Jase?" she whispered.

Dropping his hands to her shoulders, he tugged her closer. She went into his arms willingly, and, as he held her tenderly, the warmth of her was a painful reminder he wasn't dead, after all.

She stared up at him in wonderment. Did she feel it, too? Jase leaned down and touched his lips to her forehead. She closed her eyes and sucked in a shaky breath. He wanted this moment to go on forever…but too many obstacles stood in the way. And even though danger might be dogging their every step, he knew the biggest hurdle of all was the thought of opening his heart to another woman. He had barely survived losing Abby. He wasn't sure he could go there again.

Reluctantly he let her go and had started to leave when she grabbed his hand. "Jase, wait."

He turned back to her, a whisper of a smile playing on his lips.

"Please be careful. Please come back to me."

A wave of raw emotion swept through him. Her soft, plaintive words held more promise than anything had in a long time and he latched on to it like a lifeline.

"I will." He clutched her hand tight and then let it go.

FIVE

Reyna hadn't felt this way in such a long time and that scared her. It reminded her of the things missing from her life. She'd been frozen since Eddie died, her heart encased in grief. There was a time when she couldn't imagine finding another man attractive, but she definitely was attracted to Jase Bradford. Was it simply because of his connection to Eddie? The danger they shared?

It's too soon, her heart cried. *I'm not ready to let you go yet, Eddie. I miss you terribly.*

It hurt to think about moving forward. Living again. These past six months had been a nightmare of long days filled with aching loneliness, and now someone wanted her dead. She had to stay focused. Forget about what Jase had awakened in her.

Without him close by, Reyna's nerves screamed to life. Several passersby glanced her way curiously. She ducked her head, trying not to call undue attention to herself. It was Saturday and a relatively nice fall day in Colorado in spite of the snow flurries. It had tourists coming out in droves to enjoy the treasures of this quaint mountain town.

Reyna could just see inside the storage facility from

where she stood. A man seated at the counter watched the security monitor closely.

She focused on the phone. Five minutes had passed. A prickling of unease went through her. She had rented the locker from an older woman who told her she'd lived in Eldorado all her life and had worked at the facility for almost ten years. So who was the man? Maybe he was the actual owner.

Still, it didn't feel right. *He* didn't seem to fit. Reyna strained to get a closer look. He certainly didn't appear to be a local. He wore a dress shirt and pants that didn't fit with the job and he kept checking his watch. The second Jase had walked in, Reyna was pretty sure she saw him text someone. Was she being paranoid? She certainly had reason. She remembered the letter she'd mailed to Sara. Had she unknowingly sealed both their fates by sending it? If the men were monitoring her calls to Sara, chances are they were examining her mail, also.

Nine minutes gone. "Get out of there, Jase," she hissed under her breath.

When the tenth minute passed and Jase still hadn't returned, Reyna stepped out on the sidewalk. She peered over her shoulder one more time. Finally, she saw him coming from the back of the storage facility with the laptop bag tucked under his arm.

Relief coursed through her as he reached her side and grabbed her hand. "Let's go."

"What happened in there?"

"I'm not sure." His expression grim, he glanced back in the direction he'd come. "The man behind the counter seemed extremely edgy the whole time I was there. He looked as if he was expecting someone to show up. I went out the rear entrance instead. He saw me leave and started to yell for me to stop. When I didn't, I think he may have called for backup." He slid her a look. "How did you pay for the storage locker?"

They continued walking at a fast pace toward the Land Cruiser, her breathing coming in frightened gasps. "I used cash. When I opened the account, there was an older woman working the office. I've never seen this man before."

"Did you give her your name?"

"Yes," she admitted reluctantly. "It just came out before I had time to think about using another alias. I'm not used to all this cloak-and-dagger stuff."

"Did she ask to see your driver's license?"

She nodded. "She did, but I told her I'd forgotten it and she didn't push the matter. I realized I'd made a terrible mistake in giving her my name so I made up an address in another state."

"Good catch. Still, it doesn't really explain how they found out you left the laptop here."

"I think I know how," she said, and told him about her letter to Sara.

He nodded. "That explains it. They've been watching your friend closely, expecting you to contact her."

"And I did. I'm sorry, Jase. I didn't think…"

He squeezed her hand. "It's okay. You've done remarkably well for not being used to covering your tracks."

"What I don't understand is why they just didn't take the laptop. They'd have the evidence they need. Why put one of their men in the storage facility to watch for us?"

"Maybe they thought you copied the files? They would have to be certain there were no more copies floating around before…" He glanced down at her. "They can't let you live, Reyna. Even if you don't understand everything that's on the laptop, you know too much, which is why we need to get out of here now before it's too late."

Jase stopped suddenly, barring her way with his arm.

"What is it?" she asked as fear and adrenaline trickled through her. His arm circled her waist and they ducked into the doorway of a store.

"See those four men dressed in casual clothing across the street?" he asked, and she nodded. The men were talking among themselves and they watched the people passing by as if they were looking for someone. "It could mean nothing. Maybe they're simply waiting for their spouses, but I don't like it."

"Jase, they're standing between us and the Land Cruiser. If we try to get to it, they'll see us. We're trapped."

He flicked his gaze toward the men. "Maybe not. Look, they're moving. We need try to blend in with the crowd until they pass by, then we can get to the vehicle." He focused on her for a second. "Do you have any sunglasses?"

She shook her head. "No, I left them in the car."

Jase thought for a moment then pulled the hood of her jacket up. "That's better." He took out a pair of dark shades from his pocket and put them on her. "Those will hide most of your face so they can't recognize you."

The four men continued walking down the sidewalk while scanning the crowd of people as they went.

Reyna froze. They were crossing the street. In a minute, they'd be right next to them. "Oh no," she whispered, clutching his arm. He followed her gaze and saw what she did. "Jase...what should we do?"

"It'll be okay. Just follow my lead." Before she knew what he intended, Jase drew her into his embrace, leaned in close and slowly kissed her.

Reyna's breath lodged in her throat.

She forgot about the men advancing closer. The fear and dread that had been her constant companions these past few weeks faded away. All she could think about was this man kissing her. A damn broke inside of her and then she was kissing him back, all thoughts of danger forgotten.

It had been so long since someone kissed her the way Jase did. There were so many times over the past six months when she would have given just about anything for one more kiss from Eddie. One touch. But Eddie was gone and kissing Jase, feeling their breaths mingling, his lips tenderly pressed against hers, it felt almost as if she were betraying the love of her life.

Reyna jerked away. Their eyes locked. She could read all the turbulent emotion in his gaze, and yet for the life of her, she couldn't think of a single thing to say. She absently reached up and touched her lips where his had rested.

"I'm...sorry. I just wanted..." He didn't finish.

She could feel the color creeping up her cheeks. "No, it's okay." Looking away, she cleared her throat. "Do you think they saw us?"

"I don't know." He sounded as breathless as she felt. "But we need to get to the SUV while we still have the chance."

In her head, she understood that he'd kissed her to keep her identity secret. That wasn't what scared her the most. It was her reaction to it. Jase Bradford was far more dangerous to her inner peace then the men following them ever could be.

They slipped in with a group of people crossing the street. Jase tried to keep his mind on the threats facing them and not on the woman next to him, but it was a difficult task.

Just playing a part, he told himself. When he'd worked for the CIA, he'd gotten good at assuming a role. He'd even had to play the husband of a female asset once to get her safely out of a danger zone. Never had it shaken his resolve like kissing Reyna had. She felt so good in his arms, almost as if she belonged there. He had to keep reminding himself she was Eddie's widow. She loved *Eddie*. Still, the hardest part was the unwelcome memories it churned up.

Memories of Abby.

He'd thought he finally gotten over losing her. But kissing Reyna had opened a wound he wanted to leave closed. It hurt too much to think of the sacrifice Abby had made…and for what? They were still no closer to identifying the people responsible for her death than they had been back then.

"Let's hope they keep scouring the town for us, but still we won't have much time," he said in a strained voice.

As they neared the Land Cruiser, Jase's chest tightened when he saw the new threat. Two men staring directly at them. "Don't look up," he whispered close to Reyna's ear, and then he smiled down at her. "There's two men heading our way. Try to look normal. Laugh as if I've said something funny. We have to get to our vehicle. It's our only way out."

She pretended to laugh, yet he could feel her trembling. He took her hand. He'd do anything to keep her safe, to make her less afraid. She brought out the protector in him.

"Almost there," he murmured.

They rounded the front of the SUV. The two men

stopped some ten feet away and stared at them and then at each other.

Jase unlocked the door. "Get in. Hurry."

"Hey there, buddy. Hold up a second," one of the men called out. Jase didn't listen. He hopped in next to Reyna and fired up the engine.

"Hey, stop!" the man demanded once more. Jase put the vehicle in Drive and floored it without closing the door.

"That's them. There're trying to get away! Call for backup," the second man yelled.

The door slammed shut next to him as Jase turned the nearest corner. He swerved, barely missing a parked car, and then glanced in the rearview mirror. Both men had rounded the corner. They were running after them with their weapons drawn and pointed at the vehicle. It looked as if they had some sort of silencer attached to the guns.

"Duck!" Jase shouted at Reyna. He shoved her onto the floorboard as a round of bullets struck the back window, shattering it instantly.

Jase kept as low as he could and still see the road ahead. Another round of fire took out the windshield.

He drove at breakneck speed down the narrow street then turned into an alley that was barely wide enough for the Land Cruiser to make it through. The vehicle shot out the other side of the alley and onto a residential road heading out of town.

"I think we lost them for now, but we have to get off this road and out of sight. These people are ruthless and, I'm guessing, just desperate enough to risk exposure. Why else would they fire on us in the middle of a town full of tourists?"

Reyna slipped back into her seat and stared at the ruined windshield. Visibly shaken, she turned to him with terror in her eyes. "Where can we go that they won't find us?"

His thoughts circled in a dozen different directions. If they didn't disappear quickly, they'd get caught. He couldn't let that happen. He prayed desperately for guidance. It was imperative they find out what was so important that these people were willing to ambush them in broad daylight.

"The first thing we need is to find somewhere safe and secluded enough to take a look at the files. I have a friend who has a house on the other side of Silver Mountain. We're about an hour away from his place." He glanced behind them. No one followed so he slowed the vehicle's speed. "We can't afford to be out in public too long. They know this vehicle now. They'll be watching for it."

Reyna tugged her jacket closer against her body. It was freezing in the Land Cruiser in spite of having the heater blasting on high. Jase reached behind his seat, found an old blanket he kept in the back, and she wrapped it around herself for extra warmth. At least the snow had stopped for the time being. Still, they were both chilled to the bone. They needed to get out of the elements fast.

Jase spotted the remote gravel road he'd been watching for. "This will take us into Silver Mountain." He slowed the vehicle's speed long enough to type an urgent text message to his friend Aaron Foster, informing him that he and Reyna were in trouble and heading his way.

It took only a matter of seconds for Aaron to respond.

Gone abroad. House key is in the light fixture at the back of the house. How can I help?

Not exactly the news Jase was hoping for, but not totally unexpected. Since Aaron retired from Special Ops a few years back, he'd worked with the military to train other soldiers to become part of the specialized team. He was gone on average at least one week a month.

Need your expertise. Can we talk? Jase typed back.

Is this line secure?

Jase answered, Yes, it's a burner.

Good, I'll contact you at fourteen hundred hours.

Jase dropped the phone on the seat between them.

"He's not home so we're on our own for backup." He explained about Aaron's military background.

"Did you guys ever work together back then?" Reyna asked curiously.

Jase shook his head. "No, Aaron doesn't know anything about my past. We met by accident about a year ago. Aaron was looking for a hunting guide, which I do in my spare time. We became friends. We still go hunting every fall and Aaron tells me stories about his days in Special Ops. I think he suspects there's more to my story than I've told him but he never asks."

"He sounds like a nice guy."

"One of the best." In truth, Aaron was one of the few people Jase had considered sharing his past with, but he'd always held back. Now there would be no other choice. They reached the edge of the town of Silver Mountain. Jase remembered it was similar to Eldorado in layout, the main street lined with rows of tourist shops and a handful of restaurants. Instead of driving through the town, he took one of the back streets.

"Aaron's place is about as off the grid as mine. He told me once that he liked the solitude of the mountains because it helped him put things into perspective. He owns a two-hundred-acre ranch that you can only reach by driving down a ten-mile dirt road." Jase could certainly understand Aaron's need for solitude. The type of work they did made it hard to adjust to normal civilian life. Sometimes being alone was the best way of dealing with the nightmares.

Once outside of town, Jase drove slowly up the steep mountain road until he spotted the simple gate leading up to Aaron's place tucked up against Silver Mountain. When they reached the house, he pulled the Land Cruiser around behind it and parked. The seclusion of the place could prove either to be the perfect hideout or the makings of the worst ambush ever. He noticed Reyna staring at the house.

"Jase, there's a light on." She pointed at the second floor. He saw it, too. A tiny light shone through slatted wood blinds. Had Aaron forgotten to turn off a light upstairs or was someone in there?

"Stay here. Let me have a quick look around inside."

He started to get out, but she stopped him. "Jase… wait." Her voice caught over his name and he turned back. Even exhausted, she was lovely. She had the type of eyes a man could get lost in.

He gave himself a mental shake. He was getting soft.

Reyna closed the space between them and went into his arms. After a second's hesitation, he held her close. She was like a safe place in a terrible storm and he breathed in the fresh, clean scent of her. She smelled like the mountains he loved. Like a promise yet to be fulfilled.

He clung to her until she pushed away and he let her go.

"Be careful," she whispered.

"I will." With one final searching look her way, he drew the weapon and got out of the vehicle.

SIX

With the exception of the light, the house appeared empty. He hadn't seen any movement from inside.

Jase stepped up onto the deck, opened the top of the light fixture. The key had slid to the bottom.

He took it out and unlocked the door, then slipped inside. The first thing he noticed beyond the quietness of the place was that it was warm. Jase slowly crept upstairs to the room in question. He gripped the doorknob, counted to three to himself and swung the door open. The room was empty. In the corner, a tiny nightlight lit the place. He let out a huge sigh of relief and searched the rest of the upstairs. There was nothing out of the ordinary.

After a thorough search downstairs yielded nothing, either, Jase went back to the SUV. "Everything's good. Aaron just left a nightlight plugged in." He gave her a reassuring look. "We should be safe here."

Once they went inside the house and locked the door behind them, Reyna stopped in the entryway and stood perfectly still with her eyes closed. Then she looked over at him and smiled. "This feels wonderful."

He grinned at her enraptured expression. "Yeah, it's amazing the things we take for granted—like heat and a dry place to stay."

"Yes. How long can we stay?"

He wished he had a clear answer to give her. "I'm not sure. I want to get a look at those files and we need to lay low for a while. These people obviously have a lot of manpower on the ground." He glanced at his watch. "Aaron should be calling soon. I'm praying with his help we can find a way out of this."

Reyna followed him into the great room and sank down on the sofa. The crazy pace they'd been on since they left his house was taking its toll on both of them. Jase took off his jacket and sat down next to her. He wanted to be close. His desire to protect her ran deep.

"Why don't you stretch out on the sofa for a bit? Try and get some rest."

Before she could answer, his phone chirped and he picked it up. Aaron's number appeared on the screen. Jase answered the call and put it on speaker so that Reyna could hear.

"Davis, I'm hoping you made it there safely?" Aaron's booming voice came through the phone. He sounded tense, as if he were spooked about something.

Jase and Reyna's gazes locked. "Yes, we're here, Aaron. Is everything okay?"

"I'm not sure." Aaron hesitated. "I got a call from a friend right before you texted me. He's been monitoring the ham radio for a while and there's a lot of unusual chatter out there about a couple of fugitives. A man and a woman. If they're talking about you, it sounds like they're organizing a massive manhunt and they've looped in the local authorities. What kind of trouble are you two in?"

"I wish I knew," Jase told him with an exasperated sigh. "I'm here with my…friend, Reyna Peterson."

"Good to meet you, Reyna. It's a shame it has to be under these circumstances."

Reyna smiled. "Me, too. Thank you for giving us a safe place to stay."

"That's no problem. Now, what's going on, Davis, and how can I help?"

Jase realized he had to start with the truth. He just hadn't imagined how hard it would be. "Aaron, I need to tell you that my name is really Jase Bradford and I'm former CIA." He hit the broad strokes of why he had faked his death, then went on to explain about Eddie dying and the reason he and Reyna needed his help now.

Aaron blew out an audible breath. "Wow, and I thought I'd seen some bad things during my time with Special Ops. You think whatever's on the laptop is connected to what happened to your team?"

Jase furrowed his brow. It was too much of a coincidence otherwise. "My gut is telling me it has to be connected. Whatever is on it is obviously extremely important to someone."

He took the laptop from the bag and let out an admiring whistle.

"I'm looking at the laptop now. It's state-of-the-art. Looks like it's equipped with a sunlight-readable touchscreen, a fingerprint scanner and some antitheft features. It appears impenetrable, but Eddie obviously cracked the code somehow..." He glanced Reyna's way. "Any idea where he got it?"

"No, none."

Jase studied it closer. "It's military grade, but I've never known any of our people to use this particular type of laptop."

Aaron was silent for a second. "I'd need to get a look

at it. Can you use the video call feature on the phone? It'll be the next best thing to me being there."

"That's a good idea. I'll call you right back on it." Jase hung up the phone and brought up the video chat feature. While he waited for Aaron to pick up, something on the side of the laptop caught his attention. The wireless modem was disabled. There was no way to access the internet. Eddie was making sure no one could track the laptop.

When Aaron appeared on the phone's screen, Jase showed him what'd he'd discovered.

"You're right about the importance of those files," Aaron told them gravely. "Something's on there worth killing for. We have to figure out what."

Jase noticed something else. "It looks like at one time the laptop had a tracking device installed on it. Eddie must have removed it, as well."

Once the laptop was running, he saw what Reyna had told him about. There were two sets of files. "What's wrong?" she asked, noticing the taut expression on his face.

He pointed to the screen. "You were right about part of the files being encrypted. My guess is Eddie wasn't able to decode it before his death." Jase turned the phone so that Aaron could see what he was looking at. "Any ideas?" he asked.

Aaron studied the laptop for a second, then said, "I've never seen anything like it before. Without knowing what software the owner used, I wouldn't even know how to begin to crack that code. We're going to need some help."

Jase had an idea, but it meant reaching out to an old contact.

"Let's hope the second file is less complicated," he

said as he clicked on it. It contained a group of photos. There were half a dozen similar pictures showing a caravan of Humvees moving through a mountainous region.

"Why encrypt one set of files and not the other?" Aaron asked the obvious question.

Jase sat back in his chair and thought about the photos for a moment. "Because they really are two separate files. I think Eddie took the photos. He was doing surveillance on someone...or something."

The pictures were time stamped, the date more than six months earlier. Jase enlarged one of the photos. He could see inside one of the Humvees. It was loaded with weapons.

"The military wasn't performing operations in the mountains of Afghanistan at that time, were they?" he asked Aaron.

"Not to my knowledge."

Jase blew up the photo as much as he could. The driver certainly wasn't military.

"These aren't our men." He pointed to the driver, who was obviously an Arab. "I'm guessing the weapons are stolen."

He turned to Reyna. "You said Eddie was the only one from his unit who died. If the entire unit was involved in the mission, then why let them live and kill Eddie?"

"I don't know. It doesn't make sense," she said in frustration.

Jase leaned closer to get a better look at the weapons. "Aaron, that's some serious artillery they're moving."

He showed it to his pal, who studied the photo for a moment. Aaron then hissed out a breath. "It could do a lot of damage. Where do you think they're transporting them?"

Jase had spent enough time in Afghanistan to recognize the rugged mountain region. "That's near the border of Pakistan."

Aaron's mouth tightened. "Once they get the weapons over the border, there'll be no getting them back. The tribal areas between Afghanistan and Pakistan are terrorist controlled for the most part."

"Exactly." Jase brought up the next photo. It was a surveillance photo of massive amounts of weapons being stored. Jase could make out at least a dozen men moving the weapons into the building.

Reyna glanced over his shoulder. "I can't even imagine how much they've managed to store up by now. What are they planning…?" The two of them stared at each other in alarm.

"That's a good question," Jase said. "Who knows how long they've been doing this. These pictures are over six months old. In the terrorist business, a lot of things can happen in that amount of time."

"We have to find out who's behind this before it's too late," Reyna whispered. "I want to know who was responsible for taking Eddie's life." She leaned closer and studied the photo and he was aware of her in a dozen different ways. The smell of her perfume tantalizing his senses. Her warm breath against his cheek. The feel of her knee gently nudging his. He forced himself to concentrate of what he was doing.

Jase enlarged the next photo. It showed what appeared to be some type of camp in the desert. There were more than a dozen tents set up. Men dressed in desert clothing carrying various types of weapons, their faces hidden from view. He honed in on a table set up outside one of the tents. It held a dozen or more surface-to-air launchers.

"I can't believe it…" He showed it to Aaron.

"Some type of training camp, maybe?" Aaron suggested.

"That'd be my guess." Jase flipped through the pictures once more. "The question is how do all the photos fit together? And who's behind this? Without the information in the encrypted file, we're playing a guessing game." He ran a weary hand over his eyes.

Reyna touched his arm. "You're tired. You just need food and rest. You're working off sheer adrenaline alone. Maybe we should take a break. Things always look much clearer once you're rested."

He hoped she was right, but he had a bad feeling. A whole lot of people had died because of the secrets contained in those files.

He tried not to show Reyna his uncertainties. "You're right, and I will soon. In the meantime, why don't you try and get some sleep? Aaron and I will keep working the photos."

She hesitated, then said, "I could use a shower. Is it all right, Aaron?"

For someone not accustomed to being on the run, she had held up amazingly well.

"Make yourself at home. The guest rooms are upstairs. Take your pick."

"Thank you." She smiled wearily and left them alone.

Once she was upstairs, Aaron said, "You know, I was serving in Afghanistan around the time of your attack. The CIA kept a tight lid on it, but I remember hearing whispers about it from one of the men I worked with who was CIA. It wasn't right, what happened to your people."

Jase swallowed back the lump in his throat. "No, it wasn't. We lost a lot of good people that day." As always, his thoughts drifted to Abby. She was so beautiful and so intelligent. He still missed her terribly.

"I'm going to text my friend Tim. Maybe there's something new coming over the ham radio. Hang on a second." Aaron's image disappeared and Jase fought back the bitter memories once again.

It took only a matter of minutes before Aaron returned. "I don't get it. Tim said the thing was exploding with noise earlier. Now it's as if they've gone radio silent. I don't like it."

Jase agreed. "I'm going to reach out to one of my old contacts. See if we can set up a meet. He's an expert in encryption. I'm hoping he can crack the code to unlock the second file."

Aaron nodded. "Good idea. Use the Jeep in the garage. Get your vehicle out of sight as soon as you can. They'll be looking for it."

"Thanks, Aaron, I will."

"I'll have Tim monitor the situation. See if he can find out anything more about what happened there today. I'll check back with you in a couple of hours. But Reyna's right. You need some rest. You look dead on your feet."

"I will," Jase assured him before he ended the call. As much as his body craved rest, the encrypted file was taunting him with its hidden answers.

It had been years since he'd last spoken to his former linguistics professor so it took him a few minutes to remember the phone number. He typed it in but couldn't hit the call button. He hesitated to bring the danger following them to his friend's door. Unfortunately, he needed answers and they were running out of time.

In addition to being a language specialist, Bryan Northcutt was one of the best decoders Jase had ever worked with. He'd used him numerous times during his days at the CIA and Jase trusted him completely. Along with Jase, other members of the CIA routinely used Bryan's services. There was no way his old friend wouldn't know about his assumed death. He couldn't imagine what Bryan would think about hearing from a dead man.

Lord, please help us. We need Your insight and Your protection.

When Reyna came back downstairs thirty minutes later, Jase was standing by the kitchen window. His hair was damp from the shower, his shirt buttoned loosely.

He seemed lost in thought. He turned when he heard her walk in.

"Is everything okay?" she asked, because she didn't like the serious expression on his face.

He managed to smile for her sake. "Yes. You couldn't sleep?"

"No, I'm too keyed up," she told him.

"I spoke to my old college professor earlier. He's an expert at encryption. He's agreed to meet with us tomorrow morning in Aspen Grove. I hate leaving the protection of this place, but we need the rest of the information to figure out what we're up against."

Reyna wasn't sure how she felt about the news. As much as she trusted Jase to make the right decisions, the risk they'd be taking by going back out in public without knowing the full extent of the danger they faced was staggering.

Jase watched her and seemed to read all her worries.

"It'll be okay. We'll take Aaron's vehicle. They won't be looking for it."

She slowly nodded. "You trust him?"

He was quick to reassure her. "I do. You can, too."

Reyna wished that she could be as trusting, but the only person she had any confidence in now was Jase.

She noticed him favoring his left shoulder. She could tell it was still bothering him.

"Let me take a look. Make sure your shoulder's healing properly."

"I'm okay," he muttered, trying to act strong, but she could tell that stress and the lack of sleep hadn't helped much with the pain.

Reyna shook her head. "You're not. I saw a medicine cabinet upstairs. I'll see if there's something we can use. Why don't you have a seat at the kitchen table, and I'll be right back."

She didn't give him the chance to protest. Running upstairs, she retrieved some gauze, tape and something to clean the wound.

Jase struggled to unbutton his shirt, but even the slight movement was painful.

"Let me help you." She stepped close, inches from him, and he tensed. Reyna didn't look at him as she finished with the buttons, then gently slipped the shirt off.

The wound looked the worse for wear. Their time on the run hadn't done it any favors. As she worked, she was aware of him watching her closely.

"How does that feel?" she asked once she'd finished.

He reached for his shirt, winced as he put it on, and slowly redid the buttons. "Better, thanks."

She looked into his midnight-blue eyes and her chest grew tight. Their gazes tangled together. He swallowed visibly and she followed the movement.

He was so close. She could feel the warmth of his body near her. If she leaned in just a little bit she could be in his arms. Feeling the comfort of another human being assuring her she wasn't alone. She couldn't think of anything she wanted more.

Jase was still seated as his hands encircled her waist, drawing her closer. Barely five-two, Reyna was now face-to-face with him.

He tipped her chin back so that he could look into her eyes. Her breath hung in her throat. They were inches apart, close enough to kiss. Jase stared into her eyes for a second more and then he gently pressed his forehead against hers. Reyna swallowed back her regret. After a long moment he pulled away and slowly got to his feet. She turned aside to hide her disappointment.

She heard him dragging in a sharp breath. "I should go move the truck. It wouldn't do for the men following us to spot it from the air."

SEVEN

"I'll be right back…" He didn't wait for her to answer. He needed space between them to clear his thoughts.

His heart slammed against his chest at an alarming rate, his breathing shallow. What was he *thinking*? Almost giving in to temptation and kissing her again would have been a foolish mistake.

On both their parts. Because the truth was, the memory of the woman he'd once loved was always close. Abby was a tough-as-nails seasoned operative by the time they'd met. They'd worked side by side through some of the worst conditions on the battlefield. Falling for each other came naturally, and it was hard to keep their romance secret from the rest of the team. When he'd learned of her death, it had crushed him. He'd thought his chance at love had died with Abby, but as he'd watched Reyna work on his shoulder, something unfamiliar had stirred inside of him.

Reyna was beautiful and smart and so different from Abby and yet there was no denying the spark of attraction between them. The soul-deep yearning. It was as if his heart had suddenly been awakened by the warmth of her gentle touch against his skin.

Get a grip, Bradford. She's your best friend's widow.

Her life is in jeopardy. All the more reason to keep a level head.

Reyna was depending on him to keep her safe. To help her unravel the contents of the files and find out what happened to Eddie. He couldn't let himself get caught up in messy emotions.

Jase dragged a hand over the back of his neck and took a second to examine his surroundings. After talking to Aaron one thing became crystal clear. The men chasing them were coming after them full force.

He'd need to change out Aaron's license plates with his. That way if those men did find them, they couldn't trace the plates back to his buddy's home. He'd use some back roads that wouldn't be on most GPS systems to meet Bryan. They'd be safe enough.

Jase walked a quarter of a mile into the woods behind the house and the layout did little to ease his mind. Ice covered most of the ground beneath his feet, the path overgrown with trees. It was an eye-opening experience.

If they were forced to go this way, it would be a dangerous ride. Not to mention the mountain behind the place would limit their escape routes.

Jase pulled the Land Cruiser into the garage next to Aaron's Jeep and exchanged the plates. With nothing left to do, he headed back inside.

Guilt weighed heavy on his heart. They'd both just let their feelings get the better of them.

He found Reyna in the kitchen staring at the pantry.

She turned as he entered and held up a jar of spaghetti sauce. "I figured we could use a meal." She avoided making eye contact with him. The awkwardness between them still fresh.

"That's a great idea," he said, and suddenly she smiled

at him. He loved the way it lit up her face and how her eyes sparkled with newfound hope. She was infectious.

He went over to the fridge, took out vegetables for a salad and began chopping. While they worked, he snuck little glances her way. She wore her shoulder-length brown hair loose. When she moved, the light caught golden streaks. Her skin was tan. She was dressed simply in a white T-shirt and jeans that hugged her body in all the right places. He found himself wondering what she did in her spare time. Did she spend a lot of time outdoors?

"Jase?" He realized she'd asked him something and he had no idea what.

"I beg your pardon?"

She gave him a quizzical look. "I asked if you like garlic. I found some seasoning that should bring out the flavor of the sauce."

"Oh…yeah, I love garlic." *Seriously, Bradford.* Feeling the color creeping up his neck, Jase turned back to his chopping. He tried not to react when she stepped close and added the seasoning to the sauce, but he was acutely aware of every little thing she did.

Reyna worked with a skill that spoke of someone who loved to cook, and within no time, the kitchen filled with the aroma of spaghetti sauce. Once the food was ready, he carried the bowls heaping with spaghetti along with the salad over to the table and they sat down.

She bowed her head and closed her eyes, praying quietly. He reached for her hand and bowed his head, as well. Startled, she hesitated only a second, then said the blessing aloud.

"Lord, thank You for providing us with this wonderful food. For giving us shelter when we needed it most. For watching over us throughout this nightmare.

Please help us find the answers we need to understand what we're facing, but most of all, protect us as only You can. Amen."

Jase cleared his throat and dug into the spaghetti. It was nice, sharing a prayer over a meal. It reminded him of simpler times when he was a kid. His parents said blessings over their meals. It stuck with him throughout his life. Now, for just a little while, life seemed normal again. He could almost imagine them being any couple enjoying a meal together. But they weren't, and every minute they were standing still, the chances of the danger closing in on them was enormous.

"This is delicious," Jase told her.

She smiled. "Thank you. It *is* good and I don't think it has anything to do with my cooking. It's just that it's been a while since we've had anything substantial."

"Whatever the reason, I'm one happy camper." Jase dug into the meal with gusto. He tried to remember the last time he'd enjoyed a sit-down meal with someone. Sadly, longer than he could remember, and that disturbed him. Because he could get used to this, and that was dangerous on many levels, not the least being that one or both of them might not make it out of this thing alive.

"Did you always want to be a doctor?" he asked curiously.

"I beg your pardon?" She put her fork down, mostly because she hadn't been expecting the question.

"Sorry, it's just that it occurred to me I don't know anything about you beyond the fact that you were married to Eddie and you're a physician." He flashed a smile and her heart did a little chaotic beat. Why did he have to be so handsome?

"Yes," she finally said.

"Yes?" Again, that dangerously disarming smile had her thinking of things like a future.

She smiled a little in return. "Yes, I've always wanted to be a doctor. Since I was about six years old, I think."

"That's an awful long time," he said, and his gravelly tone sent shivers up her spine.

Her smile widened and she felt some of the tension slip away. He was teasing her and she liked it. "It is. I used to operate on my dolls. When I got older, I roped my friends into it. Then Eddie and I were married and we went away to school together."

"And he joined the CIA," Jase concluded. "That must have been hard. We forget sometimes how difficult our career is on the people we love."

She didn't answer right away. It had been such an adjustment. She'd been so lonely coming home to an empty house. Making life decisions alone. "It was. Eddie was gone a lot. I worried about him all the time."

He nodded and grew silent once more. She could tell something weighed heavily on his thoughts.

"What about you, Jase? What are your dreams?" she asked and regretted the question when a wintery chill entered his eyes.

Jase carried their plates over to the sink and began rinsing them without answering. After a second, she followed him, took the first dish from him and stacked it into the dishwasher. She'd been foolish to ask him about such personal things as dreams. To someone running for their life, it was hard to look beyond the moment.

They worked in silence for a while and she sensed the conversation ending, yet she wasn't ready to break the connection just yet. Talking to him reminded her of normal things. Her life hadn't been normal in a long time.

"You want to get some fresh air?" he said unexpectedly once they'd finished the dishes. "It should be safe out on the back deck."

She smiled up at him. "I'd like that."

Reyna grabbed her jacket and waited while he tucked the Glock in the pocket of his jacket, and then they stepped out on the back deck.

"Do you ever get tired of breathing in this air?" she asked in awe.

He chuckled, a deep rumbling low in his throat. "No. Although I'm sure I take it for granted a lot."

"I can understand that. We all take the things we see all the time for granted. Do you know I lived near DC for years and I never saw the Washington Monument?"

He made an exaggerated shocked expression. "I can't believe it! That's like…mandatory."

They turned to face each other and she drew in another lungful of air. Jase was inches away, an unreadable expression in his eyes. She'd give anything to know his thoughts. Reyna swept back a strand of hair from her cheek. "What about you? Did you live in DC when you were with the CIA?"

His attention shifted off to the distance and she wondered if he was thinking of the woman he'd lost.

After a moment he said, "Yes, I lived in DC for a while. I had an apartment in the city that I rarely used. Mostly I was overseas. When the rest of the team went home for a break, I signed up for another mission. I was obsessed with it. I think my life was just empty."

"Why do you say that?"

He stared into her eyes and she saw the regret in his. "Because it's true, Reyna. My parents died when I was away at college and I was sinking fast. I tried a lot of things to fill the void and ended up experimenting with every kind of adrenaline rush I could find. But nothing worked." He glanced her way and she sensed he was trying to gauge her reaction.

"Believe it or not, I did great in school. I was in my final year at Virginia Tech when Kyle recruited me into the CIA. He'd seen something in me that he thought would work well with the Agency. He was right—I excelled. I worked side by side with Kyle's wife, Agent Lena Jennings, in the beginning. I learned so much from her." A muscle worked in his jaw. "When Lena was captured and killed and her death was later traced back to a terrorist regime operating in Afghanistan, well, Kyle was devastated. I was, too. Lena was like a sister to me."

"Oh, Jase, I had no idea. So this is *personal* to you."

He stared off into the distance again, his eyes as wintry as the world around them. "Yes, I guess it is. It was so hard watching Kyle grieve. Little did I know I'd be going through the same thing soon…" His voice trailed off and he swallowed hard. She watched as he struggled to cover up his own pain. It was a long time before he could speak again. "Kyle saw how volatile the war-torn area was becoming. He came to me and told me he wanted to form the Scorpion team to help fight the rising number of terrorist groups and to prevent massive amounts of weapons from falling into the wrong hands. He asked me to be lead. I was thrilled."

His mouth twisted bitterly. "At least for a little bit. Soon, the old emptiness returned and the rush I got from the type of deadly missions we performed didn't do it for me anymore."

"What happened?" she asked.

"Kyle could see I was getting burned-out. He literally forced me to take a vacation. I had no idea what to do with myself." He laughed to himself. "I hadn't been on vacation in…well, I couldn't remember. I ended up here in Colorado. Back to where I'd grown up." She watched as he smiled at the memory. "The house was gone, but the land and the mountains were everything I remembered.

"I bought the property using the Davis alias because I knew at some point in the future I'd want to leave the CIA and come here to live. So I couldn't let my real name be associated with the property…" Several seconds ticked by. "Anyway, for the rest of my time off, I camped on the land. Then, one Sunday, I ended up at the same church my family used to attend when I was a kid."

"Did anyone recognize you?" Reyna asked, surprised.

"No—thankfully. I guess everyone from my youth had left town when the mine closed up. I can't explain it, but I felt such a peace being there. After the service was over, I just sat there soaking in the quiet and I realized God hadn't deserted me like I'd thought." He turned to face her. "I was the one who left Him."

Reyna could feel tears sting her eyes. His story moved her deeply. In a way, it matched hers. There was a time before Eddie's death that she had left God, too.

"It's funny how it takes something horrible to bring us back to Him. For me, well, my work consumed me. Eddie and I had talked about having a child one day, but we never got around to it. Our work schedules always got in the way." She stole a look his way. "Then Eddie died and my world collapsed. I couldn't function. I'd gone to church all my life, but it took losing Eddie to really open my eyes to the truth. I wasn't alone. God had been there with me through it all."

Jase tugged her into the shelter of his arms and she

leaned against him. "I know what you mean. I told God if He would help me survive what happened, I'd change my life. I'd do something to help others in need. It's not much, but I work with a group of troubled kids in town. They come up to the house, learn how to do things like chop wood, hunt, survive out in the wilderness."

She smiled up at him. "Jase, that's wonderful."

He nodded. "It's a huge blessing. I love doing it, but I think I get more out of it than the kids do at times."

She touched his cheek. She had been right about him all along. He was a knight in shining armor.

"It's getting late," she said regretfully. "I think I'll try and get some sleep. You should, too."

The morning sunshine finally broke free of the clouds when they arrived in Aspen Grove.

"That's him." Reyna watched as Jase pointed out a middle-aged man wearing a gray fedora pulled low on his head. The collar of his coat was turned up against the biting chill, and he had a laptop bag strapped over his shoulder.

Jase swung the Jeep into one of the few remaining parking spots across from the coffee shop.

There were a handful of people sitting outside the shop and probably just as many inside.

Jase glanced around. "So far it doesn't look as if we've been followed." He held her gaze. "Ready?" She nodded and he got out of the Jeep and came around to open her door. They crossed the road to the coffee shop and went inside.

The man in the hat had taken a seat at a booth in the far back corner.

As Jase and Reyna approached, he noticed them for the first time. For a moment, he seemed incapable of speaking, and then he was on his feet and he and Jase embraced warmly.

"I still can't believe it is true, but I'm so happy that you're alive." He released Jase and smiled up at him. "And you have a friend."

Jase turned to Reyna. "Yes. This is Reyna. Reyna… my good friend, Bryan Northcutt."

Bryan stuck out his hand to Reyna. "It's a pleasure."

"Thank you. I just wish it were under different circumstances."

The older gentleman nodded. "Perhaps one day it will be."

The waitress spotted them and came to the table to take their orders. "Three regular coffees?" Jase glanced at his companions, who all nodded.

Once she was out of earshot, Bryan turned to Jase. "You have something for me?" he asked gruffly.

"Yes, I do," Jase handed him the thumb drive he'd saved the encrypted file on. He'd told Reyna it was best not to take the laptop with them in case there was trouble. She understood what that meant. If caught with it, there would be no way out for them.

Bryan took out his laptop and inserted the drive into it, and then he sat back in his seat and stared at the screen in astonishment.

"Unbelievable," Bryan breathed the word aloud. "I've worked with the CIA on many cases and I've only seen this type of sophisticated encryption software used by a handful of terrorist organizations. It's extremely rare and very difficult to crack."

Reyna glanced at Jase. She could see from the tense set of his jaw that this wasn't the news he'd been hoping for. Everything, including their lives, depended on finding out what was in that file.

"But you *can* crack it, can't you, Bryan?" Jase asked pointedly.

"I can," his friend assured him. "I have every type of anti-encryption software available on my laptop, including this one. It will take some time to run the program, though. As I've said, this is very sophisticated."

"Do what you have to do. We can't leave here without it."

Bryan nodded and opened the decryption program. "Jase told me the laptop belonged to your late husband?" he asked as it began the process.

Reyna wasn't surprised that Jase had shared this information. It was obvious that he trusted his former professor.

"Yes, that's right. Eddie was killed in Afghanistan six months ago." She explained about the letter she had received from Eddie telling her about the laptop and the events that had led up to her coming to Colorado.

"Amazing," Bryan said in disbelief. "Do you think the information on this file has something to do with the attack on your team, Jase?"

"It has to. It's too big a coincidence otherwise. Something our team witnessed must have set this all in motion."

Jase explained the type of missions the Scorpions performed back then.

More than an hour had passed. Bryan sipped his coffee and continued to watch the screen as the software ground through the process of decoding.

Reyna tried to relax, but her heart was drumming a fierce beat. Every minute of it was filled with tension. Even though Jase had taken all the necessary precautions to protect them, every second they were out in the open like this was dangerous.

She glanced out the window. From where they sat, she could see their Jeep, along with several other vehicles that had been there for a while. Parked a little ways in front of them, she spotted a blacked-out Suburban like the one near her home in Texas.

"What is it?" Jase asked when she let out a gasp.

"That Suburban wasn't there earlier."

He realized it, too. "You're right. Bryan, can you speed the process up? We can't afford to be caught and you can't be seen with us."

Bryan shook his head. "Afraid not. It will take however long it takes."

Reyna said a silent prayer for a speedy conclusion.

Both Reyna and Jase kept a close eye on the Suburban. So far, no one had emerged from the vehicle. Were they waiting for them to come out to grab them?

After another half hour, Bryan blew out a shaky sigh. "I have it. I'll copy the translation onto the thumb drive. Do you think you'll need the encryption software again? I can copy it onto the drive for you. It's pretty self-explanatory."

"That's a good idea. I don't think we can risk meeting again. It won't be safe for either of us. Can you do it quickly?" Jase asked when he saw four men exiting the Suburban.

"Done." Bryan removed the drive and handed it to Jase, who slipped it back into his jacket as he and Reyna got to their feet.

"Jase, they're coming this way," Reyna whispered frantically.

Bryan rose quickly and briefly hugged Jase. "Hurry. Please be careful."

Jase didn't move right away. "You should come with us, Bryan. They might have seen us together."

"I'll be fine. This booth is pretty secluded," Bryan tried to reassure him. "Besides, they're looking for you, not me."

"Still, I'd feel better if you disappeared for a while, just in case they traced the call I made to you. Do you have some place you can go for a few days?"

Bryan smiled grimly. "I do. You and Reyna get out of here before it's too late. Don't worry about me. Call me the minute you can talk freely."

Through the storefront window, Reyna could see the four men dressed in dark clothing, sunglasses hiding their eyes, striding quickly toward the entrance.

"Let's hope there's a back exit." Jase grabbed her hand and they headed for the back of the coffee shop.

They slipped through curtains separating what appeared to be the kitchen and storage area from the rest of the coffee shop just as the four men entered the building.

A single employee, a young woman, was working dough on a floured counter. She was obviously surprised by their sudden appearance.

"We need a way out of here quickly. We're being followed. Is there a back entrance?" Jase asked her.

She hesitated for a second as if trying to decide if he were telling the truth or just some kook. Then she nodded. "Yes, follow me." She wiped her hands on her apron and led them past stacks of coffee cups to the back door. "If you go down the alley behind the building and make a left, it will take you back to the main street."

Jase stepped outside and looked around. "It's clear," he told Reyna, and she followed him. Jase turned back to the woman. "Thanks for your help. If anyone should ask about us—"

"Ask about who?" She smiled and winked at him before closing the door.

He and Reyna headed quickly in the direction the young woman indicated.

"We need to hurry. It won't take them long to realize we've slipped out the back even with our helper in there," Jase said as they raced through the alley.

Behind them, Reyna could hear the sound of someone opening a door with such force that it slammed against the outer wall.

"They had to have come this way. Are you sure you didn't see anyone leave the building?" An angry-sounding man spoke to someone.

Another voice, the young woman, answered, but Reyna couldn't make out what she said.

"You'd better be telling the truth—otherwise, we'll be back. Everyone fan out. They can't be far. Find them."

Jase and Reyna slipped around the corner and headed for the street where they'd parked the Jeep.

Once the reached it, Jase stopped and peeked around the edge of the building. "The Suburban is still there. I think there may be more people inside. We need to stay in the shadows as much as possible. Let's hope they won't see us before we reach the Jeep." A noise behind them had him glancing that way. Footsteps. The men were coming after them.

"Over there." Jase pointed to a streetlight that was out. "Let's cross here and then keep close to the parked cars until we reach the Jeep."

Reyna looked over her shoulder as someone yelled, "There they are! They're getting away! Stop them!"

Reyna and Jase raced across the road, their cover blown. Up ahead two more men exited the other side of the building.

"It's not much farther. Keep behind me. We know they're armed," Jase called as they ran for their vehicle.

Ten more feet. Almost there, Reyna thought to herself.

Jase hit the unlock button. Three cars ahead, the passenger-side door of the Suburban opened and another man wearing a jacket with something bulging from underneath headed straight toward them.

Jase lifted Reyna and all but carried her the rest of the way to their vehicle. She slid into the driver's seat and he followed. He started the Jeep and threw it into Drive, then hit the lock buttons as two of the men chasing them reached for the door handles and tried to jerk them open. Jase peeled out of the parking spot barely missing the man who had just left the Suburban.

"Get in the vehicle. Don't let them get away again," one of the thugs bellowed to his partners.

Jase floored the gas pedal and sped down the street until they reached the edge of the small town.

Reyna glanced behind them. The men had gotten into the Suburban and were giving chase. "They're coming after us, Jase! We can't go back the way we came."

Through his rearview mirror, he watched the Suburban rapidly advancing on them. "I know another way to Aaron's place, but first we have to lose them. Hang on." He jerked the wheel hard to the right and they sped onto a smaller side street and headed out of town.

The Suburban somehow managed to make the turn and was within a few feet of their bumper.

"They're going to pass us," Reyna gasped.

"They're trying to get in front of us so that they can stop us. Hold on tight."

The Suburban swerved to the left of them and tried

to pass, but Jase jerked the wheel and the Jeep blocked it from succeeding.

The passenger in the Suburban rolled the window down and pointed something at them.

Jase flicked a glance her way. "Get down. He's going to fire on us."

She ducked low and prayed with all her heart as the sound of gunfire exploded all around them. Jase swerved the vehicle from side to side. Thanks to his evasive maneuvers, the bullets missed them.

He pulled out his weapon. "I think I can take out the engine. Can you hold the wheel steady for a second?"

Reyna wasn't so sure, but she would do everything she could to help. "Yes, I think so. Go ahead." She sat up in the seat and grabbed the wheel.

While Reyna struggled to keep her attention on the road ahead, Jase leaned out the window as the driver of the Suburban joined the passenger and continued to fire on them.

Unrattled by the onslaught of bullets whizzing past his head, Jase carefully aimed the Glock and fired once. Reyna heard the shot hit metal. She glanced in the rearview mirror in time to see the Suburban run off the road and slam headfirst into a tree.

Jase took the wheel from her. "You hit it dead center," she said in astonishment.

"They won't be following us anymore, but who knows if they've called for backup. We have to disappear fast."

She looked at the wreckage behind them. "Do you think anyone survived?" Even though those men had wanted to harm them, she couldn't wish the same fate on them.

"Let's hope." He grabbed his phone and called 9-1-1. "There's been an accident just outside of Aspen Grove heading south. Send an ambulance and the police right away." Jase ended the call and dropped the phone in the seat beside him.

Reyna couldn't stop shaking. "I can't believe what just happened. How did they know where to find us?"

He slowed the Jeep's speed as he turned onto a back road. "That's a good question." He spared her a quick look. "I think they may have traced us through Bryan. If that's the case, they'll be monitoring my phone now." He rolled the window down once more and tossed the phone out.

They traveled in silence for a long time. All she could think about was how close to death they'd come once more. God had been watching out for them throughout this whole ordeal and she whispered her thanks to Him.

"Do you think Bryan will be okay?" Reyna finally asked. She couldn't bear it if she'd put someone else's life in danger.

She could see from Jase's tense profile that he didn't know. "Bryan's pretty resourceful." He turned to her and touched her arm. "This isn't your fault, Reyna. These men, they're the ones who are responsible for killing Eddie and probably the rest of the Scorpion team. They're dangerous and they're planning something deadly. They have to be stopped before they can hurt anyone else."

EIGHT

Reyna brought two cups of coffee over to the table and handed Jase one.

"Thanks." He smiled up at her appreciatively. After their narrow escape from the thugs outside of Aspen Grove, his adrenaline was working overtime. He was desperate to get back to Aaron's place and find out the contents of the encrypted file.

While Reyna settled down beside him, Jase grabbed one of the extra burner phones he'd stashed in his backpack and video conferenced Aaron to explain what had happened at the coffee shop.

"I can't believe it," Aaron said. "That's incredible. Let's hope whatever's in this file will put the pieces of the puzzle together, because so far, I have no idea what's going on."

"You're not the only one." Jase inserted the drive into the laptop and sat back, amazed. "It looks like there are several files contained within the one." He clicked the first file. The second it opened, he realized it was going to be a long day.

"What are those?" Reyna asked, her eyes widening in surprise when she saw the numbers.

Jase stared at what appeared to be a page of numbers grouped in sets of twos and then it hit him what he was looking at. "They're longitude and latitude coordinates. Hang on a second, Aaron. I need to check something on my phone."

He typed the first coordinate into the phone. "It brought up a location in Islamabad, Pakistan," he told Aaron. "Nowadays, Islamabad is a dangerous place. Terrorist groups are vying for control of the city."

"Do you think the coordinates are leading to where the weapons are being stored?" Reyna asked.

"Maybe," Jase said doubtfully. Something about that theory didn't add up. He brought up another coordinate and then it dawned on him. "They're the locations of US embassies."

Reyna shook her head. "I don't understand the significance."

Jase didn't, either.

"Why isn't the military going after the missing weapons more aggressively?" Reyna asked in frustration. "Besides the cost factor of losing so many weapons, I can't imagine what would happen if they were to be used against us."

The thought was sobering. "It could be…catastrophic," Jase said, and opened the next file. It took him a few seconds to accept what he was seeing. "I can't believe it. Aaron, I'm looking at a list of CIA safe houses across Afghanistan." How had such confidential files come to be on the laptop? The implication was terrifying. Had someone within the CIA supplied the information?

"The CIA strictly guards those locations," Aaron put in. "Their agents' lives depend on it. So how did it end up in the hands of a possible terrorist?"

"That, my friend, is the million-dollar question."

Jase's pulse pounded at the possibility of someone from the CIA being corrupt.

He opened the third file. "Oh, man, I can't believe what I'm seeing," he said in shock. "Aaron, it's a list of CIA agents working in Afghanistan." Jase recognized many of the names on the list. He'd worked with them personally.

It took a second for Aaron to answer. "Brother, that doesn't sit well with me."

Jase opened the next file and what it contained was even more shocking. "It's a list of foreign assets the CIA has cultivated since the war began. If the names fell into the wrong hands these people's lives could be in jeopardy."

Aaron let out a long whistle. "Sounds like Eddie may have uncovered a possible mole within the CIA."

Shocked, Reyna turned to Jase. "Do you really think that's true?"

"As much as I don't want to believe it, I think Aaron may be right." Jase opened the next file, which didn't seem to fit with the rest. He frowned as he stared at the information. "Oh, wow. I've seen this type of document before. When I was active, we used to get these updated lists on a weekly basis."

He showed the document to Aaron. "It's a list of the CIA's top ten terrorists operating around the world—several in the area where Eddie died. It has their aliases along with where they are supposed to be operating. Their lieutenants. Even the names of their family members. This information could be a valuable commodity to someone. The question is, who?"

"You think we have a new player in the game? Someone who the CIA doesn't know about yet?" Aaron asked. "Someone wanting to take down the rest of these guys?"

Jase hesitated. "It's possible, but I'd say it's more likely one of these guys on the list is gathering the information." He scanned the list of names. Several were dead or had been captured. Most didn't have the influence to bribe someone in the CIA to help them with their plot. He had an uneasy feeling this was the handiwork of one man in particular.

Jase opened another file and the contents all but confirmed the truth. Someone was planning a major attack.

"What *are* those?" Reyna queried as she looked at the information before them.

Jase blew out a sigh. "It's a list of the same US embassies across Europe I just looked at. Only this time the document has blueprints for the secret emergency exits and how to disarm the security systems. Other than the Pentagon, only high-ranking embassy personnel and the CIA detail attached to the embassy would have access to these." Turning toward Reyna, he gave her a grim look. "Aaron's right. Someone in the CIA is leaking this information. That explains Eddie's warning in the letter. I'm guessing the only reason the information hasn't been used yet is because it hasn't gotten into the hands of its prospective buyer. I believe we have Eddie to thank for that."

Reyna stared at him wide eyed. "I can't believe it."

"There's only one person I can think of who has enough power to either turn or blackmail a CIA agent," he said, pointing to the first name on the list. "This has to be the work of the Fox. He's planning on taking out the competition so that he can have full control of the area."

Nodding, Aaron confirmed what Jase had just said.

"Who's the Fox?" Reyna asked innocently.

"Only the CIA's most deadly terrorist leader working today," Jase told her. "He operates one of the largest cells in the world. The Agency has been tracking him for years and yet he is always just one step ahead of them. And he just happens to be the one the CIA believes was responsible for Lena's death."

"That's horrible," Reyna breathed the words aloud.

Jase considered the possibilities. What if the person who compiled the lists had intended to sell them to the Fox? The information contained there would be an invaluable asset to him. He thought about what he knew about the Fox. The man was crafty, he'd give him that.

"Why is he called the Fox?" Reyna asked curiously.

Jase ran a hand over the back of his neck. "The CIA nicknamed him that because of his ability to keep his identity secret. No one had ever seen him. He has countless safe houses spread out across several continents. He's gotten good at operating in the cloak of anonymity. He has hundreds of soldiers doing his bidding so that he doesn't have to get his hands dirty," he said with disgust. "The CIA discovered that once a soldier fulfills his mission, the Fox has them killed. His identity is kept hidden with the blood of his followers."

Reyna stared at him in horror. "He sounds ghastly. I can't believe anyone would follow such a person."

That was something Jase couldn't wrap his mind around, either. How did bad people like the Fox end up having followers who would give up their lives for him? "It's unbelievable, I know." He tried to make sense of what they'd uncovered so far. "So, if the Fox were the intended target for the information, the damage he could do would be astronomical."

"It makes sense in some weird way. Why not take out the competition and gather enough information on the CIA operatives to either kill them or avoid the areas where they operate?" Aaron surmised.

Unfortunately, Jase had to agree. He remembered something he'd read after he moved to Defiance. It was about the death of one of the men named on the list of terrorists. The CIA suspected he might have been executed by a rival terrorist group.

"Not to mention exact retribution on the assets cooperating with the CIA," he added. It certainly seemed to add up, but it was still just a working theory. They were missing a key piece of the puzzle: How did Eddie get the laptop and who had compiled it?

Jase scrolled down through the list of agent names and realized there was another page. His fingers froze on the mouse when he saw one name in particular. His. *He* was on the hit list.

Reyna leaned over his shoulder and saw what he did. Her hand shot to her mouth. "They've known you were alive all this time? Why didn't they come after you before now?"

Stunned, he shook his head, his thoughts jumbled. "I'm sure they tried. But without knowing the alias I was using, they wouldn't be able to find me."

"Until I led them right to you." She came to the same conclusion he did.

He squeezed her hand. "This isn't your fault. This has been in the works since long before you found me."

"If they've been looking for you all these years, they won't give up easily. These men are hard-core assassins," Aaron said in amazement.

Jase pointed to the name below his. "Kyle's name is here, as well. Aaron, he's my former handler. They know he lives outside DC. They even mention his sister's name. And the thing is, I haven't heard from Kyle in a long time, and when Reyna tried to reach out to him, he never called back."

"You think something's happened to him?" Aaron asked in concern.

"I don't know." His fears for Kyle's safety doubled. He couldn't believe all this time they'd been hunting him and Kyle.

"I'm sorry, Jase. I hope you're wrong. Is there anyone else? We need to get you two out of there as soon as possible," Aaron told them. "If the Fox is behind this plot, you are both in serious danger. The people chasing you can't afford to let you live even if they get the laptop back. It'll be your life or theirs."

Jase could feel Reyna's uneasiness growing and he understood why. "Jase, we can't. Remember Eddie's warning…"

He took her hands in his. "You're absolutely right. Eddie had his reasons for not wanting you to trust anyone from the government, but we need help…and I need you to trust me."

He could see all her misgivings in her expressive green eyes. After what felt like the longest moment in his life, she lifted her shoulders in defeat. "I do trust you. I trust you completely."

"Thank you," he said humbly while reciting a silent prayer that *his* trust in his former employers wouldn't end up costing them their lives.

A thought occurred to him. "Even if something did happen to Kyle, I believe the secure email address he gave me to use in an emergency will still be monitored for any activity. I know Kyle. He'll have a backup plan in place." He gave Aaron the email address. "When you contact him, type this message. 'Need something removed. Can you suggest a surgeon?'"

Aaron jotted it down and then promised, "I'll do it right after we hang up."

Next to him, Reyna tried to stifle a yawn. He glanced at his watch, amazed to find it was almost midnight. They'd been at it for hours. He was exhausted. He knew Reyna must be, too.

"Keep working, Jase. Let's pray something key will jump out. I'll try and get in contact with your former handler. In the meantime, I'll see if my friend Tim, who lives near Eldorado, can get you to a safer location for the time being. There's a landline phone on the desk in the corner. Tim's number is posted next to it. You can reach him anytime that way and it'll be the most secure way to talk. Take care of yourselves. I'd say get some rest, but we both know you need to connect the dots on those files soon or..."

Jase understood what his friend had left unsaid. His and Reyna's time was running out.

Reyna lay in bed struggling to fall asleep, but it was an elusive hope. She couldn't get Jase out of her head no matter how hard she tried and she just didn't understand it.

She shoved her fist against her forehead. "Stop it." The only thing happening between them was just the raw emotions coming to a boiling point for two people caught up in a desperate situation. Facing life and death, things came to the surface. Old longings...

The word stuck in her head. *Longings?* Why had she thought that? Jase was just trying to protect her out of a sense of loyalty to Eddie. He'd kissed her that one time because... Well, it certainly didn't feel like a man trying to comfort a woman and neither did her reaction to it. No point in denying she was attracted to Jase. Rugged, blond haired and a bit rough around the edges, he was so completely opposite Eddie in looks but so much like him in personality. They were cut from the same cloth. All the more reason she couldn't let her fascination with Jase get in the way of figuring out the truth. She owed Eddie that and so much more.

Reyna stared out the window at the night sky darkened by clouds. She felt as dreary as the world outside. She rolled on her side.

The snow reminded her of the last Christmas she and Eddie spent together. They had gone to the Wintergreen Resort in the Blue Ridge Mountains. They'd stayed in a little cabin. It snowed the whole time they were there. It had been wonderful.

She smiled at the memory. For a time during that trip, he'd been like the old Eddie. Carefree. Happy. He'd actually laughed. She couldn't remember the last time she'd seen him so content.

Reyna closed her eyes. Then he'd left and she didn't see him again until he came home on leave after his mother passed away from cancer. She barely recognized him he'd changed so dramatically.

To this day, she didn't understand why he gave up on the CIA. She had begged him to tell her why he wanted to leave. He still worked in the Clandestine Service division, but he was home every night. Why would he want to go back to a war zone? Eddie refused to talk to her about it. He'd just told her it was something he had to do.

None of her husband's actions before his death added up. After he went back on tour, every time she spoke to him he sounded more afraid than the time before, and it was as if a little bit more of Eddie disappeared with every mission.

She stared at the wall in front of her. She was so

confused. She loved Eddie, and yet she felt something for Jase. Was it just because of the circumstances they faced…or did her feelings run deeper? At this point, she wasn't sure which she wished for the most.

A noise shook him from a light sleep. Jase had fallen asleep on the sofa in the great room. He didn't remember lying down, he'd been so exhausted.

He sat up quickly and listened. It was a phone ringing. Someone was calling on the landline.

Jase went to the desk and picked up the receiver. Before he could answer, a man's voice came on the line.

"My name is Tim and I'm a friend of Aaron's." There was no mistaking the panic in Tim's voice.

"Is something wrong?" Jase asked in concern.

"Yes. I've been monitoring the ham radio for a while and you need to get out of there. They're coming for you," Tim warned. "They know where you are at. I've been trying to get to you for a couple of hours but I finally gave up. There are roadblocks everywhere and I just overheard a message come across one of the channels. They're broadcasting the latitude and longitude coordinates for Aaron's place. They'll be there soon. Get out of there *now*." Outside, a loud noise drew Jase's attention from what the other man was saying. It sounded like…a chopper.

"They're here now."

"Okay, listen to me carefully," Tim said urgently. "Aaron has a four-wheeler stashed in the red barn at the far corner of the place. If you can reach it, head east. The easiest place to cross the mountain is there. You won't be able to make it all the way over on the four-wheeler, but it'll give you a head start." He paused to catch his breath. "Once you summit, there's a ranch in the valley about five miles on the other side. It's owned by an older couple, Don and Linda Warren. Tell them Aaron sent you. They'll help you. They're good Christian folks."

Jase abruptly dropped the receiver back into its cradle and glanced up the stairs. Reyna stood at the top of them, fully dressed with the tote slung on her shoulder and fear etched all over her lovely face. She took the stairs two at a time. "What is that?" she said in a panicked tone.

He raced to the door and jerked it open. Then he stepped out onto the front porch and listened. In the distance was the sound of chopper blades cutting through the thin mountain air. He'd been right. They were almost here.

He slammed the door shut. "A chopper, and it's close. They've found us. We have to leave right now. Are you ready?"

"Yes, I'm ready."

"That's my girl." He managed a weak smile for her sake. After he stuffed the laptop bag inside his backpack, they hurried out the back door. The chopper was almost right on top of the house now. He could see the barn up ahead of them. Just a few more yards. "We're almost there," he yelled over the noise.

Reyna stared up at the sky. "I don't understand how they keep finding us."

"That's a good question." It was something that puzzled Jase, as well. Had they run every single Jeep in the state of Colorado as Aaron suggested? It was a long shot that he didn't buy. But, if not, how could they have known to search near Aaron's place? He'd destroyed both their phones. There would be no way to track her unless...

The bag.

Other than the watch, which, according to Reyna, hadn't left her possession, it was the only thing left that she'd brought with her. Jase grabbed her bag, dumped the contents and quickly searched through each item. There was nothing out of the ordinary. He picked up the bear key chain and examined it closely. On the bottom of the animal it looked as if someone had cut a hole in it. Jase ripped it open and found what he was looking for. A small tracking device. He yanked it out.

"That's how they found us. It wasn't your phone after all. They planted a tracking device on your key chain. You said they searched your house. They must have done it then." He tossed the device into a snowbank.

"Then why didn't they find us before now? Especially since we've been at Aaron's cabin for a while?" Reyna asked, perplexed as they continued to walk at a fast pace.

"The mountains have a way of playing havoc with signals, especially when the weather turns ugly like it has recently. They probably couldn't pick up the signal until now." Jase glanced up as the chopper's light found them and followed their every move. He grabbed her hand. "Run, Reyna. We have to get to that barn over there where Aaron stored his four-wheeler. It's our only chance to escape."

They had barely cleared the front of the workshop when the sky lit up like lightning and the earth around them rumbled and shook, then exploded with shock and awe.

The dust and debris from the explosion mushroomed in all directions, covering everything in an ash-gray veil. Reyna couldn't see more than the distance of her hand in front of her.

Jase.

She stumbled to her feet. Fear pumped adrenaline through her body. She'd lost sight of him in the chaos that had ensued after the explosion from above had propelled her backward some ten feet in the air. It reduced the garage and workshop that was behind the house to a pile of rubble in a matter of seconds. Reality settled in. She and Jase should be dead.

Pain shot up her arm. Her wrist was severely sprained and swelling by the second. Her hair was matted with blood, and she was scraped and bleeding in several places, but she was alive and in one piece.

She ignored her pain. All she could think about was finding Jase. As the dust began to settle, she spotted him lying in a crumpled heap a few feet behind her. She ran to his side.

"Jase!" He was bloody and lying at an awkward angle. The blast had embedded bits of shrapnel in his face. Reyna shook him hard and he opened his eyes.

"Are you hurt? Can you move?" She did a cursory exam of his limbs. Nothing was broken.

"I'll be okay," he rasped. "We have to reach the barn, Reyna—" Before he could finish, a series of explosions rocked the earth beneath them, taking out the barn. She screamed as it went up in a blaze of fire.

Reyna covered Jase's body with hers until the immediate danger had passed.

They stared at the raging inferno that had now become their world.

"Jase, they took out our only means of transportation," she whispered in dismay.

"We have to keep going. We can't give up. We can't let them win."

He struggled to stand and Reyna draped his arm over her shoulder and slowly helped him to his feet. He leaned heavily against her.

The chopper circled back around and began to search the ground below.

"We have to reach that tree coverage over there. They won't be able to find us in it. Thankfully, the backpack survived the explosions." Jase grabbed it and heaved it onto his shoulder, and then he noticed the way Reyna cradled her injured wrist against her body. "You're hurt." He touched her wrist and pain blurred her vision.

"It's just a sprain," she said through gritted teeth. "Let's keep going."

He obviously didn't believe her, but their options were limited.

The chopper's light continued to pan the surrounding area. It found them and honed in.

"Run, Reyna," Jase grabbed her uninjured arm and urged her toward the trees while the spotlight mirrored their every move.

They reached the edge of the tree line as a round of bullets fired from an automatic weapon whizzed past their heads, kicking up the ground around them. Reyna shrieked and Jase pulled her along behind him into the thick trees. He glanced up at the chopper, which had temporarily lost sight of them in the dense growth. "It's looking for a place to land. They'll have troops on the ground within minutes. Reyna, there's only one way out of here. We'll have to cross over that mountain." He nodded toward the looming monster before them.

Traversing the mountain meant they'd be facing even more treacherous weather conditions, including subfreezing temperatures, and Reyna would be going into it with an injured wrist.

She drew in a breath. The pain in her wrist had become excruciating. "Do you have something we can use as a sling? That will help keep it immobile."

Jase quickly took off his jacket and ripped part of the liner out, then tied it around her neck in a makeshift sling. "Better?"

"Much. Thanks." It actually was. She'd do what she had to do, bear the pain with as much grace as she could, because she wanted to bring Eddie's killers to justice.

"Let's keep moving. It's our only chance. As cold and as miserable as the weather is, it's probably the only reason we're not in custody or dead by now," Jase said.

God had been watching out for them. They were truly blessed to be alive.

"At least we shouldn't have to worry about them tracking us. We just have to get across that mountain somehow. There's an older couple on the other side who can help us."

That would be the hardest challenge of all. Reyna peered back over her shoulder at the death trap they'd narrowly escaped. She could see the lights of what she assumed were four-wheelers coming their way. There were men on foot, also.

Jase saw it, too. "Listen to me," he said with a raw urgency in his tone. "We have to stay one step ahead of them long enough to find out the names of the killers and bring them to justice. Can you make the hike?"

She tried to sound more confident than she felt. "Yes, I'll keep up."

He managed a weary smile. "Good. This looks like the spot Tim mentioned. It should be the easiest place to cross. We can't afford to use any lights so it won't be easy."

"It doesn't matter. Let's get out of here." She couldn't stand looking at the carnage behind them any longer.

Something akin to admiration flashed in his eyes and he smiled. "Okay. This way."

On the other side of the mountain range was another set of problems. Where could they possibly run that these people wouldn't find them?

Reyna wasn't sure which was the lesser of two evils. Staying and facing the traitors behind them or summiting that mountain range. She prayed they weren't signing their death certificates.

NINE

They'd been climbing for hours and Reyna wasn't sure how much farther she could go. She was drained and the weather hadn't let up. The wind screamed around the mountain, and several times they had to brace themselves just to keep from falling. Ice mixed with rain had long since soaked through their clothing and they were both close to succumbing to the elements. The pain in her wrist made her sick to her stomach and blurred her vision.

Jase realized she was in serious trouble. "How bad is it?"

"Bad," she said through a clenched jaw.

He pulled out his cell phone. "I'm going to try and reach Aaron. Maybe he can suggest an easier way out of here." He listened for a few minutes and then ended the call. "There's no cell service. We'll never make it over this way. We're not even halfway up the mountain." He glanced behind them. "I can see their lights. They're gaining ground. The chopper is scanning every square inch of the area, which is the only thing that has kept them from locating us before now. We have to find another way out."

Jase squinted at the face of the mountain. "Wait, I

think I see something. It looks like a small opening in the mountain." He pointed to it and Reyna tried not to get her hopes up. "It looks like a mining shaft, maybe. We can take shelter in there for a bit. Hang on a second and I'll check it out."

Jase went into the opening and she waited outside. He came back in a matter of minutes. "It's not much, but it's our only option right now. You need to rest your wrist and we both need to warm up."

Reyna had only been in a couple of caves in the past exploring with Eddie. Being in an enclosed area normally gave her the creeps, and as she followed Jase inside, she tried not to freak out too much at the scurrying sounds around her.

"I'm going to do my best to conceal the opening. At least give us a fighting chance. I'll be right back," he assured her as if sensing her uneasiness.

With Jase gone, Reyna tried not to lose control. She counted off the seconds. One. Two. Three.

"That should keep them from spotting it. I'm hoping they're not going to expect us to summit the mountain but find an easier way out," Jase said as he came up behind her. He retrieved his flashlight and flipped it on. "Let's see how big this thing is." He headed deeper into the cave and Reyna clutched his hand and was practically glued to his back. Jase stopped abruptly when she let out a frightened yelp as something ran across her foot.

He reached up to steady her. "He's probably more afraid of you than you are of him. Chances are they haven't seen a human around these parts in years."

She was behaving like a child and she knew it. They had been running for their lives for hours; they'd narrowly escaped death many times, and she was going to freak out about a few rats? Still, she gripped his hand tighter. He laced his fingers through hers and shone the light down a narrow passage. "Some of these old mines can go on forever. Maybe the people who operated it made another way out of here."

The passage was so low that they had to bend over to walk. Reyna could feel the walls closing in.

They'd gone a short distance when the pathway dumped into a large open area. The ceiling above them had to be more than fifteen feet tall. She breathed a huge sigh of relief.

"This will do," Jase said, shrugging off his backpack. "We should be safe here and no one from outside will spot a fire. I'm going to see if I can find some wood. You rest your hand."

For once, she was happy to oblige. She sank down against the rock wall. "How are you holding up? Are there any residual effects from the explosion or your shoulder injury?"

"No, I'm fine. And I must say, both of you are looking pretty good, considering."

She sat up straight and stared at him. If he were seeing double, then he could have a serious concussion and...

He laughed and she realized he was teasing her. Trying to lighten the moment.

"Sorry. Bad joke. Even worse timing. I'll be back in a jiff."

She smiled up at him, then relaxed against the wall. She couldn't believe what had taken place over the past forty-eight hours. She thought she'd been so careful. Using a disposable phone, borrowing Sara's car, and yet they'd known where she was all along using a simple device placed inside her key chain. It was terrifying how unrelenting these criminals were.

"I found some usable firewood." Jase came back carrying an armful of it. "Who knows how long it's been sitting here, so let's hope it lights." He stacked wood into a pile and then fetched some paper and matches from his backpack. It took only a few minutes for the fire to catch. Satisfied, he nodded. "The only problem is the wood is dry, so it'll burn fast, but there's lots of it. I'm thinking the miners spent the winter up here."

Reyna inched closer to the fire. It was blissfully warm. "I can't imagine living in such primitive conditions during the winter."

"Yeah, those old-timers had to be tough to survive. We should be safe for a little while. Let me have a look at your wrist."

He squatted next to her and gently unfastened the sling from around her neck.

"They know we're still alive. They're not going to stop until they kill us." Reyna barely got the words out. She was beyond exhausted. She couldn't imagine how Jase must feel.

Their eyes met and held. "They're going to try. I'm not going to let that happen."

Her head swam. "How can they simply explain away what happened here tonight? Won't people question it? I mean it's a virtual war zone back there."

"They are good at making people and things disappear," Jase said, clenching his jaw. "They've killed before many times and will sweep this under the rug. Make up some story—perhaps say it was a lightning strike that started the fire. Those things happen up here all the time. No one will be the wiser."

"They're going to try and blame this on Eddie, you…me."

"Not on my watch. Eddie wasn't a traitor and neither

are you. We just have to find the missing piece that will help this make sense. Without that information, we can't tie the documents to the Fox if he is the one behind this. We can't even prove there's a threat. We need a name."

She hated the frustration she saw in his eyes. She wished there was something more she could do to help. "I know."

"Did Eddie ever mention what his unit was doing prior to his death?"

"No, and I asked. As I said, he had changed. When he came home for his mother's funeral..." She stopped, the memory still painful.

"I'm sorry," Jase said, sympathy flickering in his eyes. "I didn't know she had passed. Eddie told me about the cancer..."

Jase's concern touched her profoundly. He was such a caring person. It amazed her how someone who had been through so much had managed to keep a gentle side.

"Thanks. Like I mentioned before, when Eddie came home for her funeral, he was like a shell of the person he'd once been. He was so afraid, jumping at shadows. He kept calling someone. When I asked him who he was trying to reach, he wouldn't tell me. He just kept repeating that if anything happened to him, I needed to come find you." Hitching in a breath, she leaned closer to him. "He told me that at least a dozen times or more. When it came time for him to return to duty, I could tell he didn't want to go."

"Do you think Eddie might have been trying to reach Kyle?" Jase asked, and she could see the thought troubled him.

"He never said. He just shut me out." Reyna shook her head. "Jase, do you think those men back there are

CIA?" There had to be a reason for Eddie's cryptic warning. "Did Eddie's own people end up taking his life?"

"I don't want to believe it, but whoever's behind this has to have a contact within the CIA. How else would they have gotten the names of agents and the locations of the safe houses?" Exhaling roughly, he scrubbed a hand over his face. "We have to figure out who's behind this, Reyna, and we don't have much time."

He grew silent for a moment, then reached out and gently examined her wrist. "It doesn't look too bad. If we had something to wrap it with, that would help."

"It won't stand up to another day of hiking. We need to find another way off this mountain." She voiced what they both knew.

Jase nodded solemnly. "You're right." He removed his jacket again and tore off more strips of cloth. "Let me know if this is too tight." Taking one of the strips, he wound it carefully around Reyna's wrist. "How's that feel?"

She flexed her hand. "Good."

He tied the sling around her arm once more. She was exhausted and discouraged, and, try as she might, she couldn't keep those things from showing. She hated revealing any weakness. In the operating room, she was fearless. But here, she was way out of her league.

"We can't keep fighting them, Jase. *I* can't keep fighting." Tears sprang to her eyes. She didn't have the energy to stop them.

"Hey…" He cupped her face and brushed away her tears with his thumb. "Don't give up, Reyna. We're not finished yet. I'm not going to let them get away with what they've done. I just need you to keep fighting."

As she looked into his piercing blue eyes, she believed him. Jase was a true patriot. If he was willing to lay down his life to save hers, she owed him the same determination. "I'll do my best."

He smiled and her heart did a crazy little flip. It had been so long since she'd felt this way. This breathless new feeling of falling... She caught herself before she could think about love. She wasn't ready yet.

Her friends at church told her that when it was the right time, she would know. But she hadn't expected the moment to come with Eddie's best friend. The timing was terrible. They didn't even know if they would make it out alive.

As she continued to look into his eyes, she wondered if he experienced the same undeniable attraction for her that she felt for him. She believed so. It was there in the way he looked at her. If only she felt this way at a different time.

He glanced away and she could breathe again.

"What I don't understand is why it took them so long to come after me. The laptop's been out of their control for six months. Obviously, the files are important to them. Why wait so long?"

Jase thought about it for a second. "I'm guessing they have been searching for it. Maybe they believed the laptop never made it out of Afghanistan. It was a bold move on Eddie's part to smuggle it out of the country when he went on leave. Once they realized the laptop wasn't in the country anymore, they were just desperate enough to come after you."

It made sense. Reyna shivered as she remembered the threats they'd made. The accusations about Eddie.

Jase changed the subject. "This mine goes on forever, but it's traveling at a downward angle, so that's something. I'm thinking the miners who worked it made another way out of here. I can't see them climbing down the way we came. In the meantime, we need to get our energy levels up." He dug into his bag and pulled out a couple of energy bars and some bottles of water. "We have to try and conserve the water as long as we can, so take small sips."

Reyna opened one of the bottles and drank. She took a bite from the bar and couldn't remember the last time anything tasted so amazing.

Jase patted the ground. "I realize the rock floor is kind of hard, but you can use the backpack as a pillow. Get some rest. I'm going to explore the cave. See how far the trail goes back." He picked up the flashlight. "If you hear anything strange, grab the laptop and come find me."

The light from the flashlight bounced off the stone walls, creating exaggerated shadows all around.

Jase struggled to combat the paranoia, the fatigue. He needed something to keep him focused. He went back over the file information in his head. As much as he didn't want to believe it, the facts were clear and staring him in the face. Someone with high-level clearance within the CIA was dirty. He thought about the lack of warning from Kyle. Was it possible...? He dismissed the idea completely. He knew his former handler the same as he had known Eddie. They were both honorable men without compromise. He needed to stay focused on getting them off the mountain and to the Warren ranch. Then he'd take another pass at the files. Maybe he'd missed something the first time and there was still one file left to examine.

Jase heard a noise up ahead. It sounded like rushing water. He stopped to listen and realized it was coming from a smaller shaft that veered to the right. It barely looked wide enough to move down comfortably. He stooped low and headed toward the sound, then stopped short when he saw what looked like a boarded-up section of the mountain.

An unsafe mine shaft? Maybe that portion had collapsed and the miners had simply boarded it up for protection?

Jase grabbed the first board and pulled hard. It came free easy enough, but the force of the movement sent rocks and dirt crashing down on top of him. The place was definitely unsteady.

He pried a couple more boards free until he had a small opening then he kicked the rest outward until he was able to see. Fresh mountain air poured in. Jase eased through the opening. It took a second to try to regain his bearings. They were at the base of the mountain range. They'd managed to find a quicker route across the mountain.

"Thank You, Lord." It never ceased to amaze how God watched out for them.

He retraced his path back to Reyna. She'd fallen asleep. He felt even guiltier at having to wake her. Staring down at her for a moment, he reveled in her beauty. He could almost imagine what it might be like, if circumstances were different, to have someone like her to rouse with a gentle kiss each morning.

But those sweet thoughts had no place in the here and now. If God was willing, perhaps someday.

He shook her gingerly.

She woke the second he touched her arm. "Is someone here?"

He could see the panic in her eyes and he was quick to reassure her. "No, we're safe. I found a way out."

She quickly scrambled to her feet and dusted off her jeans. "You did? That's great. Let's get out of here."

He chuckled at her enthusiasm. "Hang on a second, darlin'. I want to see how close the men following are getting." He slipped outside. A thick fog had the entire mountain encased and he couldn't hear the chopper anymore. The fog had grounded it. He peered through the soupy mess and saw lights off in the distance heading in the opposite direction. Without the tracking device, the thugs were going on instinct alone. The obvious path for Jase and Reyna to take on foot would be to head toward the small town of Sandy Creek.

He blew out a relieved sigh. Another blessing.

Jase went back inside and told her where he thought the men were heading. "It will take them most of the night to reach Sandy Creek and hours to search the entire town. We have some breathing room." He grabbed the map from his backpack and did a quick assessment. "From what I can tell, we're only a couple of miles away from the Warren ranch. As much as I hate involving them in this ordeal, we're both half-frozen, not to mention exhausted, and we're going to need some means of transportation out of here."

Reyna followed him down the narrow shaft and he stepped outside. "Give me your hand," he said. She linked her fingers through his, then stepped out beside him. "The fog is definitely working in our favor," Jase said, glancing up at the night sky. "With the mountain's size, the chopper will be grounded until it lifts and it's stopped sleeting for now. That's something. And at least we're heading downhill and the trail seems pretty tame compared to the route we were on."

She smiled bravely. "I'm good with tame."

Jase liked her ability to find the humor in what had

otherwise been a terrifying ordeal. They had both been through so much and she'd kept up with him all the way.

"To tell you the truth, me, too. This has been a wild couple of days. Unfortunately, I think what's ahead of us will make the last few days look like child's play." He could see the notion terrified her. "You shouldn't have to go through this, Reyna. You're an innocent. You don't deserve what's happening to you."

Compassion filled her eyes and she stepped toward him and stroked his tense jaw. "Jase, you don't, either. Eddie told me many times the work you did in those war-torn areas saved lives for both the citizens living in the region as well as Americans. You, Eddie and the rest of the Scorpions were doing good. Preventing future disasters. These people's agenda is just the opposite. They're out for themselves and their own glory."

Jase covered her hand with his and watched as her eyes grew dark with emotion. She edged nearer and suddenly the danger and the past were the last things on his mind. She was so close. He could read all of her doubts because he shared them. Felt all that pain and uncertainty with every fiber of his being. And if he moved just a smidgen, he could kiss her lips…and, oh man, how he wanted to kiss her.

He'd thought about it since their last embrace. It was undeniable that he found her beautiful. Fact was, he hadn't let himself connect with another human in such a way in a long time. Even his relationships at church were distant ones. But Reyna was strong and sweet, the type of woman a man could fall in love with, and he knew he was on the precipice.

She's Eddie's widow. She came to you for help. "I'm sorry," she said, and he frowned.

"For what?"

"For dragging you back into this mess," she whispered. "I—I wish there had been another way."

"No, Reyna. Don't be." His face contorted with pain as he fixed his gaze on hers. "I've always known this ordeal wasn't over for me, but *none* of this is your fault. I care about you and I don't want anything to happen to you…"

She stared into his eyes. "I care about you, too," she said simply. The promise of those simple words scared the daylights out of him.

He cleared his throat, his voice still a bit rusty. He pointed down into the valley. "I see house lights. That has to be the Warren place. We're almost there. The sooner we're out of the open the better."

TEN

They reached the valley floor and Jase spotted the house. He stopped a little ways from it, his heart thundering in his ears. His greatest fear was that they might be walking into a trap. After what they'd just been through, he'd learned anything was possible.

He found a group of spruce trees and stopped. "Why don't you wait here just to be safe and let me scope it out?"

She grabbed his arm. "Jase...be careful."

The worry on her face touched him to the core. "Hey..." He brushed a thumb across her cheek. "I'll be okay. We're going to get through this, Reyna. I'm not going to let them get away with what they've done. They need to pay." He smiled tenderly and added, "I'll be right back, okay?"

She slowly nodded and returned his smile and his heart did a crazy little flip. The time they'd spent together had shone a light into the darkness of his empty life. He wasn't sure he could go back to simply existing.

He turned away and headed for the house before she could see the struggle going on inside of him. Jase quickly covered the distance and stepped up on the porch.

Nothing appeared out of the ordinary. The porch was lit up and he could see a light on inside the house through the lace-curtained windows. A silver-haired woman sat on the sofa knitting. An older man was nearby in a chair in front of the roaring fire, reading a book. They seemed harmless enough.

Under his breath, Jase said a quick prayer and knocked on the door.

A handful of seconds ticked by followed by footsteps, and then the older man opened the door. He was dressed in a plaid flannel shirt, his steely eyes a contradiction to the smile on his face.

"Evening," he said, and after a quick assessment of Jase, he held out his hand. "I'm Don Warren. I imagine you must be Jase Bradford. We've been expecting you."

Jase clasped the older man's hand. "That's right. Boy, am I glad to see you."

Don chuckled and opened the door wider. "I'm sure. Aaron's buddy said you've had a tough few days. I spoke to him earlier. Where's your friend? He said you'd be traveling with a woman."

Jase pointed back in the direction he came. "I wanted to make sure everything was on the up-and-up. As you said, it's been a rough couple of days."

Don gave a terse nod. "I can certainly appreciate that. You come over the mountain range behind you?"

"Yes, that's right."

"That's a hard hike, especially at night. You both have to be exhausted. Linda is keeping a meal warm for you. Let's get your friend and get you both warm and dry."

To Jase, it sounded like sheer bliss. He motioned for Reyna and she came to where he and Don waited.

"Reyna this is Don Warren, Aaron's friend."

Don shook her hand. "It's a pleasure, ma'am. Come inside and meet my wife."

They stepped into the house, where a petite woman waited with a welcoming smile on her face.

"Welcome to our home. You two must be half-frozen. I have some extra clothes that should fit, so let's get you into something dry. There's a fire in the living room. When you're done, come warm yourself by it. I'll get supper on the table."

"Has there been any word from Aaron?" Jase asked Don once they'd finished the meal. Reyna glanced up from helping Don's wife, Linda, clear away the dishes. She could hear the tightness in Jase's tone.

"No, not a word, but I suspect the weather is playing havoc with the signals again."

Reyna bit her bottom lip. They were both so tired. The thought of having to leave again made her want to weep. As a physician, she knew they couldn't keep up this pace much longer.

Jase held Reyna's gaze. "As grateful as we are for your help, we're putting your lives in jeopardy every moment that we're here. We need to keep moving."

Linda handed him a cup of coffee. "You both are exhausted. What you need is to rest."

The thought of sleeping in a soft bed sounded wonderful to Reyna.

"She's right," Don said. "You'll be safe here. There's no way a four-wheeler can make that trek over the mountain. Not to mention they won't be expecting you to have crossed it, either. Aaron's friend said they had a chopper. It'll be grounded until morning."

Jase visibly relaxed. "You're right, I know. We've been running for so long that I'm not sure I know how to have downtime."

Don chuckled kindly. "I get it. You're afraid to let down your guard even for a second."

Reyna accepted the cup of piping-hot coffee from Linda. "We're so grateful to you and Don for taking us in."

The older woman patted Reyna's arm. "It's no problem at all. We're always happy to have young folks around. Let's go into the living room where it's warmer. It seems like each year winter comes a little earlier and stronger to the valley."

Her husband took their cups of coffee and they went to the living room. "I've got news for you, Linda. It isn't the weather, it's us. We're getting older and it's harder to endure the winters."

Reyna watched as they sat side by side. When they looked at each other the love they shared just radiated from them. It made her almost envious. She and Eddie had once had such a connection, but his years working for the CIA had changed him. He had secrets. Parts of his life he couldn't share with her. In those last few months before his death, it had taken a toll on their marriage.

Reyna shook off those dark memories. She didn't want to remember Eddie like that. She wanted to hold on to the good times.

She stole a glance at Jase. She could see the physical exhaustion etched on his handsome face, yet he wouldn't give up. He was a strong man. The time she'd spent with Jase had made her aware of the things Eddie's death had taken from her. As she studied his strong profile, she could almost imagine what sharing her life with him would be like.

He looked her way and their eyes met. His curious, searching hers for answers. She sucked in a breath. It would be so easy to fall in love with him. She was just a breath away from it now.

As his gaze slid over her face, she could feel the color rising in her cheeks, and she looked away.

Linda patted her husband's leg. "That's true, dear." Reyna realized she had no idea what Don had just said.

She cleared her throat and tried to ignore the man seated next to her, but it was a near-impossible task. She was aware of every breath he took. Every movement he made.

"Do you and Don live here alone?" she asked to take her wayward thoughts off Jase.

As Reyna was quickly discovering, Linda was a warm woman who loved to smile. "Oh, yes. In fact, we've lived most of our married life right here in Painted Rock Valley. We bought the place when Don left the service. That's been…what?" She glanced at her husband. "Forty years now."

Don nodded. "Forty wonderful years. And to think it almost didn't happen." He chuckled at the memory.

"Oh, you." Linda pretended to smack his arm. "But you're right." She grinned up at her husband. "Don asked me to marry him at least a dozen times before he left for active duty in Vietnam. I told him I wasn't ready. That I'd wait for him. We'd be married when he returned." Linda's eyes grew misty and Reyna felt as if they were outsiders in Don and Linda's world. The two could almost finish each other's sentences. It made her want a love like that. One that could endure just about anything. "Only Don was injured in battle and he almost died. I thought I would lose the love of my life." Linda shook her head. "I asked God to heal him. I told God if He would, I'd marry Don the day he was discharged from the hospital. And He did."

"He sure did," Don added with a smile meant only for his wife.

"We've been so happy. I wouldn't trade a moment of it." She dabbed at her eyes and Don tugged her into the shelter of his arms.

Reyna could feel tears close, as well. She glanced up at Jase. The tenderness etched on his face touched her profoundly. He reached for her hand and held it, and she was happy just being close to him. She'd worry about the future once they could catch their breaths long enough to think about it.

"What my wife is being so sentimental about is we've been debating on whether to sell our spread and move to a warmer climate."

"Oh, no, I'm so sorry. That must be a difficult decision for you both. Do you have children somewhere else?" Reyna asked.

Don shook his head. "We were never blessed with them ourselves, but for almost thirty years we ran a ranch for troubled youth right here, so I guess you can say we have thousands of kids." He beamed at his wife.

"That's true," Linda agreed.

"Over the past few years though, it's gotten to be too much for us. We closed the ranch down a while back and we've been living here alone ever since. We have our friends—Aaron is like a son and we love our church. But it's time to make a decision about our future. My arthritis grows worse with every passing year and I'm not able to care for the place like it needs."

Linda squeezed her husband's arm. "It's hard. But look at us prattling on and you two are ready to drop from exhaustion. When we built the ranch, we set the place up to be a series of small cabins, including ours. Don and I put you two in our most secluded cabin."

Don took his wife's hint. "That's right and I have a truck that we use to do work around the ranch. You two take it. You'll need a way out of here come morning. Linda and I have some food boxed up for you to take along with extra clothing. It's not anything fashionable, but it'll do. You both look as if you're traveling pretty light. Let's get you settled into the cabin so you can get some rest."

"Thanks for the truck…and the hospitality," Jase told Don as he clasped his hand warmly.

"You're very welcome. If you need anything at all, or if something comes up during the night, just call. I'm still a pretty good shot." Don gave him another one of his rugged mountain man stares.

Jase chuckled at the older man's directness. "We will."

They waved goodbye to the Warrens and went into the cabin. "This will do," Jase said as he closed the door and glanced around. The rustic cabin consisted of a large open kitchen, a great room, the bedroom and a small bathroom. "I'll take the sofa," he volunteered when he correctly read Reyna's hesitation.

"You don't have to do that."

"No… I insist. In all honesty, I'm too keyed up to think about sleeping."

She sighed wearily. "Same here. I'm ready to drop from exhaustion, but I'm wide-awake. I need something to do. I think I'll carry in the food and put it away."

"I'll help you. I need to bring in the backpack."

Once they'd toted in their things, Jase set the backpack on the table, took out one of the covered dishes from the box Linda had packed, and placed it in the fridge. He watched as Reyna grabbed some bread and put it in the pantry. Even worn-out and disheveled from their treacherous climb, she was beautiful. Her silky golden-brown hair fell across her face as she worked. He remembered the feel of it against his fingers. The way her eyes shone when he kissed her. He gave himself a mental shake. Best not to go there right now.

Once they'd finished putting the food away, they sat down together on the worn leather sofa. He could see something troubled her. It didn't take long to find out what.

"Jase, what happened in Abudah? What went wrong? Eddie didn't like to talk about it but I know it tormented him." He could feel his expression turn stone hard. It happened every time he thought about those days. He had finally gotten to where the nightmares were seldom. In his book, that was a good thing.

She watched as he fought back his troubled memories. "I'm sorry. Forget I asked," she said in a barely audible voice, then got to her feet to leave. He caught her hand.

"No, don't go. It's okay," he said huskily, drawing her back down beside him. "It's just hard talking about it at times. I haven't spoken about it since I came back to Defiance." His gaze met hers. "But I want to with you."

Her heart beat an unsteady rhythm. *I want to with you.* She hadn't expected those words to thrill her so much.

She sat perfectly still, riveted by the dark, enigmatic expression on his face.

"It was a setup right from the start. We went into that building to extract an asset. A woman, the wife of a high-level enemy leader operating in the area. She had information about the Fox. She agreed to talk in exchange for immunity. Only there was no one there. And we were ambushed." A muscle clenched in his jaw.

"You think someone tipped the enemy off?" She asked incredulously.

"Without a doubt. Reyna, these people are ruthless. They were determined to take out the remaining members of the Scorpions and they didn't care who they had to kill in the process. Eddie was just collateral damage," he added slowly. "The only question is who tipped them off. Until all of this started I never would have considered that someone from the CIA might be dirty. Now…" Jase blew out a breath. "That night in Abudah, well, I've gone over every part of it a dozen times in my head. As I said, the mission was off from the start. Something about it didn't feel right."

He had her full attention. "Like what?"

"For starters, normally when we went out on a mission, we were backed up by a team of marines. I can count on one hand the number of times that didn't happen, and those were always highly classified and critical missions. Then there's the fact that usually we had several hours at the very least to prepare. Not this time. We got the word we were heading out fifteen minutes before we left."

Reyna shivered at the implication and he continued, "At the time, I never questioned the order, even though it hadn't come through Kyle. I was told the mission couldn't wait. We'd gone radio silent, which was routine. I later learned from Kyle that he'd found out the mission was a setup and tried to call it off, only it was too late."

Jase drew in a breath. Let it go. "Somehow, we got separated. Abby and I were together, but it felt like we were being cut off deliberately from the rest of the team."

Reyna could see the fear he'd experienced reflected on his face.

"I was shot in the chest first. When the bullet hit my leg, I dropped to the ground. I lost visual on Abby. I could see the enemy descending…" He stopped, dragged in another breath. "They were armed to the teeth with US weapons."

"You think the weapons were part of the ones that had gone missing?" she asked.

"Probably. Anyway, before they reached me, your husband showed up, took out several of the enemy in the process, and pulled me out of there. Eddie found a safe location to leave me and then went back for Abby. She was injured, as well. He had just managed to get her out when the place exploded." Jase stared straight ahead, his voice a hoarse whisper. "No one else walked out of there alive. Brady and Douglas, our two newest members, died instantly. I guess they were collateral damage, too."

He swallowed visibly. "I was hurt bad. They didn't know if I would survive the flight to the States, but I did. I found out after I'd returned home that Abby never made it out of Afghanistan. Her injuries were too severe. She died that same night."

"Oh, Jase." She touched his arm gently.

He struggled to regain his composure. "I wouldn't have survived if it hadn't been for Eddie getting me safely out of there. I'll never forget what he did. Eddie was one of the good guys. Truly good. I'm just sorry the CIA changed him for the worse."

The raw hurt she saw in him sliced through to her heart. She looked up and found him watching her. He brushed a strand of her hair from her eyes, his fingers resting on her cheek. She could feel the solid warmth of him close to her. Smell the fresh mountain air that clung to his skin.

Jase stared into her eyes as he brought her slowly into his arms and kissed her long and slow. He wasn't Eddie. He didn't feel like Eddie, didn't kiss like Eddie, and yet she wanted to be near him. Wanted him to keep on kissing her. Wanted…

"I'm sorry…" He started to pull away. "I don't know what's wrong with me."

"No, Jase." When he would have moved away, she wrapped her arms around his broad shoulders and kept him close. They both had loved Eddie. She just needed to be close to someone else who grieved for him, too, she told herself. Still, the possibility for the future hadn't seemed this bright in a long time.

Jase froze for a second and then held her tight, and everything was right with the world for just a little while.

She looked to him for reassurances and his eyes softened as they settled over her face. He kissed the top of her head and let her go.

Jase got to his feet and stepped away. "You want to use the shower first?" he said without looking at her.

The moment may have passed, but the way she felt about him hadn't. "Thanks. After what we've been through tonight, a shower sounds wonderful."

He smiled at her. "Take your time. I'll check around outside and I'll be back in a minute."

ELEVEN

Jase stepped out onto the porch and his hands shook. He was definitely losing his edge. He'd known Reyna only a matter of days, yet he could feel a little bit of his resistance slipping away with every smile. Every sweet, disarming look she gave him. Something he never thought possible was happening, and it terrified him.

He was falling in love with Reyna.

Jase sighed heavily. She had only been a widow for six months. She might not be ready to love again. He wasn't even sure he was. Trying to solve the secrets contained on the laptop had brought a lot of old feelings to the surface. It reminded him of how deep his love for Abby still ran. You didn't just stop loving someone because they weren't with you any longer.

He circled around behind the place, then glanced back at the mountain they'd crossed. No lights showed. Hopefully, they'd be long gone from here by the time those goons discovered they'd been had.

When he went inside, he found Reyna freshly showered and setting on the sofa. She'd changed into a pink T-shirt Linda had lent her and a pair of jeans.

Jase noticed the way she favored her arm. She had taken the bandage off when she showered.

"How's the wrist?" he asked.

"It still hurts, but it's better, I think."

"It probably needs to be rewrapped after our adventure of trekking across the mountain. It will help if you keep the wrap tight…" He stopped and grinned at her. It was getting easier to find reasons to smile when he was with her in spite of the ordeal they were going through. "Listen to me. Trying to tell a doctor how to do her job."

She laughed and he loved the sound of it. "It's okay and I get it. You're used to taking care of yourself."

"Yeah, I guess you're right. I'll see if I can find something to wrap it with." He went over to the kitchen and found a dish towel. Reyna was right. He'd gotten good at taking care of himself, but having her care about him was something he could get used to.

She held out her wrist for him to examine. While he worked, Reyna found herself drawn to him. Something she hadn't experienced in a long time. His hands were rough from working outdoors. His skin tanned. Tiny lines fanned across his eyes when he smiled. She had never seen such piercing blue eyes before. They seemed to hold his secrets close. She'd give anything to know what he was thinking, but just like Eddie, he hid behind a fortress of pain.

He scraped back a lock of sun-streaked hair that fell over his forehead and looked up. Their eyes met. Held. The liquid heat in his gaze slipped over her face, melting the chill within her that had nothing to do with the temperature. These past six months, well, she'd felt as if she'd been drowning in grief. Fear. Hopelessness. She didn't feel that way any longer.

Embarrassed, she glanced away and focused on Eddie's watch on her left wrist. Even though it didn't keep time anymore she wore it for sentimental reasons. Having it close was like keeping a piece of Eddie with her constantly. It served as a reminder of the sacrifice her husband had given for his country, and for her. Eddie had loved her with all his heart and here she was having feelings for another man. A part of her felt as if she was betraying her husband's love.

Reyna looked more closely at the watch. She realized something she hadn't before. The crystal was cracked.

"Oh no," she exclaimed. She couldn't believe it had broken.

Jase saw what she did. "It must have happened during the explosion."

"I guess so. With everything going on, I never noticed it before." She took it off and squinted a little closer. "Jase, it looks like there's something behind the face."

She shook the watch and she could hear something rattling inside.

Jase held it up to the light and gingerly removed first the crystal then the face. The inside workings of the watch were missing. "That looks like the tiniest thumb drive I've ever seen. This has CIA technology written all over it."

"How do you think Eddie ended up with it?"

"I don't know." Jase took out the drive and examined it. "Eddie must have hidden it there before he died."

Their eyes met. The information on the drive had been important enough for Eddie not to want it to fall into the enemy's hands.

Jase sat down at the kitchen table and inserted the drive into the laptop. "Let's see what's on here. I have a feeling it may be our missing piece of the puzzle," he said as Reyna took the chair beside him. He could feel her warm breath against his face. Kept remembering the way she felt in his arms, the sweet touch of her lips against his, and it was impossible to shove her out of his head.

When the contents of the drive came up, it was both simple and shocking. A single photo that was different from the previous ones in content and quality. Jase could only guess that the grainy photo had been taken with Eddie's phone. The photo was of some type of compound. A prison maybe?

There were people in the photo. A woman dressed in the garb of the nomad tribes of the desert so all that showed was her eyes. Something about them seemed vaguely familiar, but he couldn't be sure why. Had he met her in the past during his time with the CIA? There was a man standing near the woman. Jase couldn't see the man's face—he was staring at the woman. Still, he appeared to wield a whole lot of power. Others close by with weapons appeared to be guarding her along with the man. Who was he? Who was *she*? Did the presence of guards lend credence to the theory of a prison?

"Do you recognize either of these people?" Jase asked.

Reyna studied the photo, then shook her head. "Not really, but it's hard to say. The photo quality is poor. Who do you think they are?"

He glanced at the woman in the photo again. "I'm not sure." Why did she look so familiar…?

Jase remembered what Reyna had told him Eddie had said. *Tell him I'm sorry I wasn't able to prove what happened.*

"Do you think this photo is part of the proof Eddie was talking about when he spoke to you last? Was your husband trying to figure out what happened to our team?"

She nodded. "Possibly. It certainly makes sense."

He studied the photo closely and saw something he hadn't noticed before. The woman was armed. She wasn't a prisoner at all. The man next to her appeared to be Arab. He was smiling at the woman as if they knew each other. The woman's skin appeared tanned from her time in the desert. She could be Arab but Jase wasn't so sure.

Still, she reminded him of…

"I don't get the connection, but it's late and we're both exhausted. Let's try and get some rest. Hopefully, things will look different in the morning. I'll just take a quick shower and then the room's all yours."

From the bedroom, Jase heard the bed squeak followed by silence. Once Reyna had fallen asleep, the quietness of the cabin settled around him and still he wasn't able to relax.

As a distraction, he grabbed his phone and checked to see if there was service yet. The weather had played mayhem with it for hours. He barely had one bar but it was more than he'd seen all night.

He dialed Aaron's number and through the crackling of the bad reception, his friend picked up.

"Jase, I glad to hear from you. I've been so worried. I've tried to reach you for hours and wasn't sure you and Reyna made it out safely. I spoke with Tim."

Jase breathed a silent prayer of thanks. "We did but just barely. I received Tim's call a few minutes before men in a chopper opened fire on us. We made it out, but they destroyed your garage and barn along with the workshop. I think it was deliberate."

"They want you alive for now. They can't kill you until they get what they came for, and they need to find out who else you've told about the files. They'll keep coming after you, Jase. And when they get what they want…"

Aaron didn't need to finish. He didn't need to. Jase understood. Once they had the laptop, he and Reyna would be expendable.

The phone lost service again and he had to redial.

"Were you able to reach Kyle?" The words rushed out. He needed to make the most of the service they had.

It took Aaron so long to answer that Jase wondered if perhaps the call had been dropped again. "No. I sent your message to the secure email address you gave me. There's been no answer. I'm not sure how much longer we should wait for the Agency's help."

The lack of contact from Kyle wasn't a good sign. And that, coupled with the length of time it had been since he'd last heard from his friend, caused Jase's bad feeling to double. He didn't want to think about Kyle being dead, but there was a very real chance it could be true.

"You're right, we can't hold off much longer. We'll need to find another way out of here."

"And I can help with that," Aaron assured him. "I spoke to my former commander. He knows what's going on and he's agreed to send in a team of Special Ops to extract you and Reyna. And guess who gets to lead them?" Through the static on the line, Jase could just make out Aaron's chuckle and he was happy to join in.

"I can't think of anyone else I'd rather have on my team."

"Happy to hear it. We just have to figure out where and when. Our window of opportunity is limited. There's another winter storm on the way and it looks like it's going to be worse than the last. It's supposed to hit sometime midday. When it does, we won't be able to get a chopper airborne to get you out." Which meant he and Reyna would be in this alone.

Jase pulled out his map and scanned it for possible locations. "There's an old military base north of Steamboat Springs. If I remember correctly, it's been deserted for years now. We'll meet you at the landing strip."

"That'll work." Aaron paused a second and Jase could hear him talking to someone. "We're looking to meet at ten-hundred hours. That work for you and Reyna?"

He checked his watch. It was just past four in the morning. The base was two hours away. If they left early to take in the possibility of bad weather, that left them with several hours to survive before leaving for the meet. "We'll be there."

"We can't wait long," Aaron warned. "If you're not there by half past the agreed-upon time, we're going to assume something went sideways."

Jase understood what that meant. There'd be no exit plan. No help.

"In the meantime, stay safe. This is almost over, I promise," Aaron assured him.

"Roger that." Jase disconnected the call and breathed a sigh of relief. It felt as if a weight had lifted from his shoulders. They just had to stay hidden a little while longer.

He rubbed a hand over his weary eyes. If they survived this nightmare, he knew in his heart he didn't want to let Reyna go.

There was no denying his feelings for her were growing. But did she feel the same way? She'd been through more than most people went through in a lifetime and she was still processing it. Was it too soon? He prayed not, but only God knew.

He glanced out at the dark night. He was exhausted down to his very bones. Today promised to be another difficult day and he needed rest. Who knows what they'd encounter on the drive to the base tomorrow.

He stretched out on the sofa and put the Glock under the pillow next to him. Still, his thoughts wouldn't shut off. The past was right here with him taunting him like a puzzle he couldn't solve. He was haunted. By the unsolved questions concerning the attack. The identity of the woman and man in the photo. But mostly by his attraction to Reyna.

Jase spent the rest of the night fully clothed, snatching moments of sleep only to awaken from dreams of Abby. At times, she appeared close enough to touch. He'd reach for her only to have her turn into Reyna before his eyes.

He wasn't sure when he had finally fallen asleep. The last time he looked at his watch it was after six in the morning. He awoke just as the first bit of sunlight edged its way through the curtains in the room and he finally abandoned sleep entirely.

Jase stretched and winced at a couple of new aches and pains. He glanced at himself in the mirror in the living room. The past life he'd lived as a spy showed on his face every day. Each death-defying mission, each kill, had left its indelible mark in the etched grooves around his mouth, the squint lines around both eyes. The furrow between his brows. He prayed with time the memories of the things he'd done in the name of justice would fade.

She had slept like a rock. Exhaustion had a way of doing that to a person. The smell of fresh brewed coffee awakened her, calling out to her from a deep sleep.

Reyna grabbed the clothes Linda had given her and went to shower. She looked so pale. The past six months had taken their toll on her emotionally and physically.

She dressed quickly and followed the smell of coffee to the kitchen. Jase was there. He stood with his back to her, staring out the window. Tall. Strong. Handsome. Dressed in a flannel shirt and jeans, he looked so good.

She must have made some sound, because he turned to her. She could feel her cheeks growing hot under his probing gaze. He took his time looking away. He'd seen something in her expression.

"Coffee's fresh. Want some?" She nodded and sat down at the table.

Jase poured a cup and brought it over to her.

She cleared her throat. "Thank you." She felt awkward with him and she wasn't sure why. What had changed? Was it him—or her feelings for him?

"There's been news from Aaron. He's assembled a team to get us out of here. We're meeting him at ten." Jase quickly ran through the details. "Soon we'll be safe and hopefully we'll be able to figure this all out."

And when it was over, where did that leave them?

When she couldn't formulate an answer, he came over to where she stood. "We're almost there, Reyna. We just have to keep fighting for a little while longer." When he gazed into her eyes, the intensity in his expression took her breath away. He looked like he was going to kiss her, and she wanted it as much as she wanted her next breath. She wanted…his heart.

Her hands cupped his face, drawing him down to her level. She yearned to feel the gentle press of his lips against hers. But it was not to be. Jase simply tugged her up and into his strong embrace. Her head resting against his heart, Reyna could hear its thunderous beat. It was just the two of them facing an uncertain future.

He let her go. He looked into her eyes and said, "You once asked me what my dreams were. Well, they're simple. I want a chance at a future beyond living in the shadows. I want to feel normal again. I want a chance to…love again." His voice cracked and she could see the fierce longing in his eyes. "I want to have a family, Reyna," he declared fervently. "I want what you do. I think we both deserve it."

Reyna's breath stuck in her throat. She did, too. She hadn't realized until she met Jase just how desperately she wanted all those things. Their gazes lingered. She'd give just about anything if they were having this conversation as two normal people not running for their lives. It was a bittersweet feeling to know she wanted love again and knowing that they may not live long enough to see if there was a chance for them to be together.

"We should collect our things. I want to be on the road soon." His voice was still a little unsteady. She understood. She felt it, too, but she wasn't ready to send the moment.

He moved away and she reached for his hand. "Jase."

He turned to her. "What is it?" he asked, and he looked so tormented. As much as she wanted to, she couldn't give him any promises just yet.

"Nothing. Only, I'll be so happy when this is all nothing more than a nightmare."

TWELVE

The noise of a vehicle approaching had Jase rushing to the window. *Please don't let them have found us again.*

He saw Don hurriedly coming up the steps. Jase unlocked the door and stepped aside to let the gentleman in.

"You folks had better get out of here as soon as possible. Linda had a call from one of her friends in town. She said there are men all over the place going door to door. They claim to work for some government security agency. She said they were flashing pictures of a couple. Linda asked her to describe the people in the photo and they matched you and Reyna. Linda's friend said it just about scared her to death." His craggy face filled with concern, Don glanced from Jase to Reyna. "They'll be coming this way soon."

Jase drew in a ragged breath. This wasn't the news he wanted to hear. What happened if they didn't make it out in time?

He dug into his backpack where he had stashed an extra phone and thumb drive. He took out the drive and copied the files on the laptop to it and then typed a brief message explaining as best he could what had happened. Jase handed the drive to the old gentleman.

"I need you to do me a favor. Can you mail this to the US Attorney's office in DC? Make sure you don't put your name or address anywhere on the envelope and try not to mail it near here. I want to keep you and your wife out of this as best as I can for your safety."

Don stared at him in shock. "Sure thing." He shoved the drive into his pocket.

"Thank you," Jase told him solemnly. He and Reyna would forever be indebted to Don and his wife. "Since we can't go through town, is there another way out of the ranch? We need to reach the old military base near Steamboat."

Don rubbed his chin as he thought about it for a second. "Yep, there sure is. You just follow the main road out of the ranch until you reach an intersection. To the right is Painted Rock. To the left a smaller gravel road. Just keep on that road for about ten miles, maybe a little more, and it will dump you onto a paved road." He paused, took a deep breath. "When you reach the pavement, you'll be just outside a small town called Jackson Valley. You can pick up the highway leading to Steamboat there." Don headed for the door. "I'd better go. Linda was pretty shook up by the call."

Jase followed him and clapped a hand on the older man's shoulder. "Thank you, Don, and thank Linda, as well. I hope we haven't caused you too much trouble by being here."

Don was quick to reassure him. "No, sir, there's no trouble. I don't like it when people try to bully other people." He nodded at Reyna one more time. "You folks take care."

Jase closed the door and turned to face her. "Are you ready? We need to get out of here before they get to the ranch."

"Yes, I'm ready," she said in a tight voice.

They went outside and Jase scanned the area for any possible threat. "I don't see anyone, but we still need to hurry."

Their breath chilled in the air as they loaded stuff into the truck and got inside. It felt as if the temperature had dropped even more.

Jase eased the truck down the slippery drive and out to the road.

They reached the intersection Don had mentioned without trouble and Jase turned left. He glanced at Reyna. He could see the uncertainty etched on her lovely face.

"Hey, it's going to be okay. This is almost over." He hoped to console her, but in truth his internal radar was going crazy.

She tried to smile, but he doubted if either of them believed what he'd said.

With nothing left to say, he focused on the road ahead while his thoughts raced over the files, jumbling things up. Confusing details. He couldn't deny the woman's resemblance was uncanny. That photo got to him because it reminded him of… *No way.*

Abby was dead.

He blew out a breath. Was he just so exhausted that he was grasping at straws?

What then was Eddie trying to tell him? The photo *had* to be important. Why else would he go to such great lengths to get that photograph to Reyna? He shook his head. Soon, with God's help, they'd be in the presence of others with whom they could examine the evidence thoroughly.

The gravel road ended outside of Jackson Valley and they picked up the highway from there.

"Not much farther," he told her. "It's only about five miles to the base."

Turning toward him, she gently squeezed his bicep. "I am so ready for this to be over."

He smiled at the way she enunciated every word. "Me, too. I want to start living again without looking back over my shoulder. I've almost forgotten what that feels like."

She didn't answer, but she was still smiling and it held so much promise.

Jase glanced in the rearview mirror and frowned. A vehicle was coming up behind them. Still some distance away, it could just be some innocent traveler.

Reyna noticed it, as well, her gaze locked with his, and he quickly tried to reassure her. "We don't know it's them. It could be anyone. Besides, they don't know what we're driving and they certainly can't know about the meet up."

She nodded but the fear didn't leave her face.

The vehicle, a large SUV, continued to keep the same amount of distance between them, almost as if they were deliberately trying to fake them out. If it was the men chasing them, he couldn't lead them to the meeting place. It was too risky. Jase had seen firsthand the manpower this group possessed. Aaron's team wouldn't stand a chance.

"I'm going to try something. See if they follow." He turned off onto a smaller road. The SUV did the same.

"They're still behind us," Reyna whispered. "How did they find us? There's no tracking device left."

She was right. How *did* they know their whereabouts? He didn't believe it was just a coincidence that the men hunting them had ended up on the same road leading to the base.

His mouth thinned. "Aaron's the only one who knows where we're meeting and I trust him completely."

"I do, too," she assured him. "Do you think someone who helped Aaron organize the rescue might be part of their team?"

It was plausible. "I'm going to see if I can contact Aaron and let him know we have a tail. Maybe he can delay leaving or at least send help." Jase called Aaron's number, but the call didn't go through. He checked the service bar on his phone. It was nonexistent. "There's no cell signal. I don't like it, Reyna. We can't lead them to Aaron's team. There could be a bloodbath."

She glanced behind them once more. "What do you want to do?"

"We've got to lose them before we get there." He glanced at his watch. It was already the scheduled meet time. They had half an hour to spare. "Aaron's team won't wait much longer. There's a bad storm moving this way, and if we're not there soon, they'll have to leave."

Jase spotted a four-wheel-drive path up ahead and to the right. "Hold on," he told her as he whipped the truck onto it and floored it. The SUV did the same, confirming the truth. This was no innocent bystander. These were the men who had been chasing them. They'd found them again.

Reyna clutched the grab handle of the truck and stared straight ahead, all color gone from her face.

The tire chains spun out of control in the deep snow. Jase's hands grew sweaty on the wheel. The SUV was now right on top of them. It rammed the truck hard. Jase fought the wheel but, with the snow and ice accumulation, he had almost no control. The truck slid sideways.

One of the men in the SUV shot out the driver's side

tires. The truck ground to a halt. Reyna screamed and squeezed her eyes shut. They were stranded up here with a group of cold-blooded killers and the worst part was no one knew where they were.

Two men got out of the SUV and ducked behind their open doors, weapons aimed.

Jase pulled out the Glock. "Reyna, I need you to do exactly what I tell you. I'm going to do everything in my power to get us out of here alive, okay?" Silently he prayed he could make good on that promise.

"Get out of the truck with your hands up!" one of the men yelled.

Reyna fearfully glanced Jase's way. "What do we do?"

"We do as they say. Stay close behind me. We're going to pretend to go along with their plan." He tucked the Glock behind his back and they got out.

Jase put his hands up and started walking toward the SUV.

"That's close enough," the man called.

Behind him, Jase heard Reyna gasp.

"Are you okay?" he whispered.

"That's the man from my church. That's Frank." Her voice shook with the revelation.

Frank grinned nastily when he realized she had recognized him. "That's right, Reyna. You should have gone along with the plan. None of this would have happened if you had. But you got suspicious." He shrugged. "I should have realized the wife of a former CIA agent wouldn't be an easy mark. You figured out I wasn't there to be your friend...and now you and Bradford are going to pay the price. Get your hands up," Frank barked at her.

"You were watching her. Trying to get her to tell you where Eddie left the laptop," Jase surmised. He needed to keep the man distracted while he figured out how to neutralize the situation. It was just the two men. If he could manage to disarm one of them, then he could deal with the other.

"Well, aren't you the master detective," Frank said in a sarcastic tone. "Yeah, Bradford, I was watching her. It was my job to make nice. Get her to trust me and then get the laptop." He waved the gun their way. "Just think how much trouble you could have saved yourself, Reyna, if you'd just talked to me," Frank mocked. "Now do as I said and put your hands up." He was growing more annoyed, so Reyna complied and lifted her hands into the air.

"That's better. Too bad you weren't as obliging when I was going to your church. You and Bradford are in a world of trouble. You're going to regret the day you met me." Frank motioned to his partner. "I'll cover you. Get him under control first. I'll take care of her." His threat was unmistakable: Jase and Reyna were not supposed to walk out of this alive.

The partner didn't like being ordered around by Frank. "Why me? You take care of him."

Frank's anger exploded. "Do as you're told unless you want to end up with the same fate as them."

Reyna inched closer. Jase could feel her warm breath against his neck. She was trembling and terrified.

"It's going to be okay. Trust me," he murmured so that only she could hear. *God, please guide our steps.*

The second man reluctantly left his hiding spot and moved cautiously toward them. He stopped a few feet away and tucked his weapon behind his back before ordering, "Keep your hands up. Don't try anything, Bradford, or I promise I'll kill her." He glanced back at his partner, who was now standing behind the SUV's door. "You got me covered?" he asked.

Before Frank had the chance to answer, Jase snatched the man's arm, twisted it behind his back and clenched it as tight as he could.

The man yelped in pain. "Let me go!" he demanded furiously while trying to free himself. Jase tightened his hold and the man slumped against him.

Using the disabled man as a shield, Jase swiped the man's weapon and handed it to Reyna. "It's loaded and the safety's off. Just point and shoot." He removed his Glock and aimed it at the man near the SUV while keeping pressure on his prisoner.

Frank didn't flinch at the sight of the weapon. "There's no way out of this for you," he said. "We have more people on the way here now. It's over, Bradford. Give us the laptop and we'll make sure your end isn't so painful. Otherwise…" Jase didn't believe a word of what the man said. The sneer on Frank's face assured him they'd be dealt with in the worst possible way.

Jase didn't respond to the man's threat. "Put down your weapon if you want your partner to live."

Frank actually laughed. "You think I care about him? I have orders to get the laptop and take you two in dead or alive. Him, I could care less about." Before Jase had time to process the threat, Frank fired at his partner, hitting him in the leg. He screamed in agony and dropped to the ground at Jase's feet.

"Frank, why'd you do that?" he raged while grabbing his injured leg.

Jase realized Frank would stop at nothing, even harming his partner. "Run, Reyna. Get behind the truck," he commanded while he aimed at Frank's weapon and fired. The gun bounced from Frank's hand and he screeched in pain before ducking beneath the door. Jase fired again and the bullet splintered the window. With his weapon still drawn, he advanced on the SUV. His training had taught him to strike while you had your enemy on his heels.

He reached the spot where Frank had been seconds earlier only to find he was gone. The adrenaline rush of being back in the line of fire had him gasping for breath. Jase slowly moved to the back of the vehicle. Suddenly, Frank jumped from a crouching position and lunged for the weapon, hitting Jase full force. He teetered backward but somehow managed to keep his footing while the man continued to snatch at the Glock in his hand. They wrestled back and forth for its possession, but Jase kept control.

Frank jerked one hand free, drew back and slugged Jase as hard as he could in the jaw. The pain was staggering, but he somehow managed to keep his wits about him. Jase shoved at Frank's chest with his full strength and sent him reeling backward onto the snowy ground.

Frank quickly bounced back onto his feet and he raised one leg, intending to strike a blow. Jase jerked to one side just in time to avoid the disabling kick. Jase could tell he was well-trained in hand-to-hand combat.

Frank's face contorted in fury that his move hadn't resulted in the desired effect. He lunged for Jase once more, his arms outstretched. Jase caught his right hand and jerked it behind him, throwing him off balance. From nearby, Jase heard Reyna scream and his heart thundered against his chest. Had the second man gone after her? Was she hurt? He had to deal quickly with Frank so that he could help her.

Jase wrapped his free arm around Frank's throat and held on tight. It took only a matter of seconds before he was out cold. He laid Frank's body on the ground, grabbed his weapon from where it had flown, and raced toward the sound of her voice.

"Reyna? Where are you?"

"Over here," Reyna managed, and then screamed again. "Help me, Jase. He pushed me over the edge of the mountain," she said in a frantic tone. "Hurry, I—I can't hold on much longer."

He spotted the injured man leaning over the mountain's edge. He was trying to pry Reyna's hand free.

With a low growl, Jase grabbed the man up by his shirt collar and punched him hard in the face. He dropped like a rock to the ground unconscious, then Jase got on his knees and knelt close to Reyna. She was dangling off the side. If she lost her precarious hold, she'd plunge some fifty feet to the bottom of the valley.

She glanced up at him with stark terror in her eyes. "Help me, Jase. I'm… I'm losing my hold."

Lord, give me the strength to pull her up, he silently prayed.

"I'm going to get you out of there, but I need you to relax," he said with as much calm as he could muster.

She was crying from fear, but as she looked into his eyes, she slowly nodded. "I'll try."

"Good girl. I'm going to pull you up, but I need you to grab hold of my hand with one of yours."

She frantically shook her head. He couldn't imagine how frightening it was to hear that the only way to be saved was to let go of the one thing keeping you alive. "No, Jase, I can't. I can't let go. I'll fall."

He held her gaze. "I'm not going to let that happen, I promise. I need you to trust me, Reyna. We have to get out of here before the rest of the thugs arrive. Please trust me not to let you fall," he said hoarsely.

After what felt like an eternity of his heart slamming into his chest, she pried one hand free and he grasped it as tightly as he could. Reyna screamed when her hand slipped for a second in his, and then she was kicking and flailing in the air.

"Jase, help me." She looked at him desperately, her eyes pleading to live.

He needed to calm her enough to pull her up. "Reyna, I've got you, sweetheart. But you have to be as still as you can."

After another tense second went by, she visibly forced herself to relax.

"Good. That's good." He smiled gently down at her. "On the count of three, I'm pulling you toward me. Ready?" She finally nodded.

"One. Two. Three." With both hands on hers, he pulled with all his might and lifted her off the side of the mountain and up into his arms.

THIRTEEN

Reyna clung to him and he held her tight. She couldn't believe how close to dying she'd come.

"You okay?" Jase whispered roughly as he stroked her hair. His voice held so much tenderness. She pulled away and looked into his eyes. The one thing that kept her from giving up while she was hanging there was the thought of him. She believed she'd been given another chance at happiness with him. She wasn't about to let these horrible men take that away from her.

She smiled genuinely and nodded. "I'm alive, so I'm okay."

He returned her smile and her pulse beat a crazy rhythm. "Good. We need to hurry, though. We might still have a chance at meeting Aaron."

Jase glanced at the man who lay unconscious behind him. "We'll take their SUV. I'll leave them in the truck. Once we're safe, I'll let Aaron know where to find them."

She watched as Jase went over to where Frank lay by the SUV, just beginning to regain consciousness. Jase grabbed him by the arm and lifted him to his feet. "Who are you working for?" he demanded.

Frank glared at him. "You're wasting your time. I'm not going to help you."

Jase dragged him over to the truck. He found a piece of rope in the bed and secured Frank's hands, then he put him in the cab and tied him to the steering wheel.

Once he was satisfied Frank was no longer a threat, he slammed the door and came over to where Reyna knelt in front to the wounded man.

She had just begun to examine his leg. "Don't try to move," she said, and gently pushed him back down when he would have sat up.

He stared at her in shock. "You're going to help me?"

He saw her as the enemy and wasn't expecting her to show kindness. "Of course. You're hurt," she told him simply.

Dumbfounded, the man slumped back against the ground while Reyna gingerly pushed his pants leg up and examined the wound.

"How bad it is?" Jase asked while he kept a close eye on Frank.

"It's not bad. The bullet didn't do much damage. It missed hitting a major artery by inches, though. Thankfully, it took a clean exit." She glanced up at Jase. "It could have hit you."

"But it didn't," he assured her. "Can he make it without further medical attention?"

Reyna ripped pieces of the man's shirt and snugged it tight around the wound. "For a while. This should stop the bleeding."

When she had finished, Jase helped the man to his feet and led him over to the truck.

Once he'd secured his hands to the grab handle, he said, "If you talk, it'll go easier for you. Tell me who's behind this."

Satisfied he wasn't going to die, the injured man smirked at Jase. "You think I'll help you? I'd be a dead man. So will you and the lady soon enough. They'll have a dozen men here soon. You can't run forever."

"Yeah, well, you and your partner will be here waiting for them when they arrive," Jase bit out, and then retrieved both men's phones. "You'd better hope our people get to you before yours—otherwise, I wouldn't want to be in your shoes."

He took the backpack containing the laptop from the truck and he and Reyna got into the SUV. He slowly eased it back down the trail and retraced their path until they were on the road leading to the base.

Reyna saw him check his watch. "Are we too late?" she asked.

"I don't know," he admitted gruffly. "I hope not, because it may be our only way out of here." The clouds had continued to gather in the morning sky and a dusting of snowflakes had begun to blanket the windshield. "I'm pretty sure those men were correct, though. They'll come here soon and they'll know we got away."

The reality of his words set in. "Jase, when he shot that man…" Tears filled her eyes. "I was so frightened. I thought you were next. I thought I'd lose you."

His thumb brushed away the tears from her cheeks and he held her gaze a moment longer. "Eddie was blessed to have you in his life, Reyna. You're strong and courageous and—" He jerked in a breath. He'd almost laid bare his heart.

"I loved Eddie so much," she said softly, and each word was like a knife. "He cared so much about you, Jase. Now I understand why. I…care about you, too." She hesitated and he hung on each word. "Being with you these last few days, well, you've made me feel special. Important. I haven't felt that way in a while."

His chest contracted at those sweet words. He wanted her to know how important she was to him, too. "I feel the same about you. You've made me realize how empty my life has been." She took his hand in hers and kissed his palm. They smiled at each other because there were no more words needed. If God granted them the future, it was full of promise, in Jase's book.

Almost there. It was almost over. He couldn't let his guard down for a minute, though. Too much was at stake.

His favorite verse from the Bible came to mind. The one about those who wait on the Lord shall renew their strength. He needed God to renew his strength right now because they were both running on empty.

Jase grabbed his cell phone and tried Aaron's number again. This time, it went straight to voice mail.

He didn't like it. How had the men found them? Was it possible someone Aaron trusted was corrupt? His uneasiness increased tenfold.

He slowed the SUV's speed to a crawl when he spotted a faded sign for the base.

"I think we should go the rest of the way on foot just in case."

He parked the vehicle off the road and behind a dilapidated building. They got out, bundled up in their coats and started walking. Jase took out his cell phone and dialed Aaron's number once more, but the call didn't go through. The phone's service was nonexistent. As they walked he mulled over the two men who had followed them. He didn't believe for a second that they had accidentally happened upon them. Did they know about the meet up? What if they were walking straight into an ambush?

"Is everything okay?" she asked in a worried tone.

It was hard to reassure her when he his own nerves were creating a storm of doubt. "Yes. There's no cell service through here." He felt a stab of guilt. He couldn't bear it if his mistake ended with her getting hurt.

"Jase…what's wrong?" she asked point-blank.

He turned away from her searching gaze. "Nothing. I'm just ready for this to be over."

She blew out a long breath. "Me, too. I'm not cut out to be a spy."

Jase tried to smile as he glanced up. Dark, threatening clouds had begun to gather in the sky above, making it appear almost dark. The snow continued to fall harder and in the distance, a bolt of lightning lit up the sky. The storm was moving in quickly and the weather was deteriorating. They didn't want to be out here when the skies opened up full force.

He gently tugged her closer. "We'll get through this, Reyna. We will. And when we're on the other side…" He didn't finish. He leaned in and pressed a soft kiss against her forehead.

In the distance, thunder rolled across the horizon and he let her go. "We should keep moving. How are you holding up?"

"I'll be fine. You don't have to worry about me."

The edge of the storm caught up with them as they drew close to the edge of the base. Ice mixed with the fat flakes of snow fell harder and he feared their window for extraction had evaporated.

Jase stopped and gave her a hard look. He needed her to understand the importance of what he was about to say. "Reyna, listen, I need you to stay behind until I've had the chance to scope things out. Make sure everything's safe before you go in."

Her reaction wasn't unexpected. "No, Jase, I won't."

She never broke eye contact. "You could be killed. I don't want you to go in there alone. Tell me what I should do."

He framed her face with his hands. "I need you to stay behind, Reyna," he repeated. "We could be walking into a trap and I can't risk something happening to you." He drew in a long breath. "And if I don't come back, take the laptop and go back to the SUV." He dug into his jeans pocket, produced the keys and handed them to her. "Get out of here as fast as you can and get the laptop to the US Attorney's office."

She stared at him with a mixture of horror and disbelief.

He gathered her close. "Promise me, Reyna. Do that for me if I don't make it out. Show the US Attorney what we've deciphered. Tell him what we suspect. Don't let *them* win."

Tears filled her eyes and she whispered, "I will, I promise."

He smiled at her answer. "Thank you. Are you ready to finish this?"

She returned his smile. "Yes."

They reached a group of run-down buildings that looked as if they had once been the base housing. Jase was on edge and second-guessing his decision to leave Reyna here alone. He prayed he wasn't making the worst mistake of his life. What if they found her first?

He spotted one of the houses still mostly intact. "Wait here and give me a second to check things out inside. If you see anything out of the ordinary, come get me."

He took out his flashlight, drew his weapon and went inside. He shone the flashlight around. It didn't look as if anyone had been in there in years. He took a quick look around and then went back outside.

"You should be safe here." She followed him inside. He opened his backpack and took out an extra flashlight and the spare phone he'd brought with him and quickly programmed in his cell number and Aaron's.

"Keep this with you but don't try to call me. It should take me about another fifteen minutes to reach the airstrip. If I haven't contacted you by then, get out of here." He handed her the laptop and swallowed hard. "You won't have much time before the brunt of the storm hits. The SUV should stand up to a lot of weather so you'll be okay. Whatever you do, don't stop. Keep moving."

They stood facing each other and for the life of him, it felt as if he wouldn't be seeing her again, and that terrified him more than anything.

"Jase, please be careful." She reached for his hand and he drew her into his arms, gathering her close. "Promise me, you'll stay alive. For me."

He held her tight and everything around them faded away. She was the only thing that mattered to him.

"I'm so sorry, Reyna. I wish I could take it all away. Erase the bad things that happened over there. Change the way the last three years went. Eddie's death…"

She nodded against his chest. "I know but it's okay. It makes me realize we're not promised tomorrow. In spite of everything, you and I are blessed beyond measure and I don't want to take a moment for granted."

She looked up at him with tears in her eyes.

He framed her face with his hands once more. "You don't do that. Of all the people I've met, it's easy to see you appreciate every moment God provides you."

A tiny sob escaped as he leaned down and his lips brushed hers. She kissed him back with urgency in her touch.

But there were things he needed to say. He couldn't

leave them unsaid, knowing he might never see her again. He ended the kiss, stepped back and drew in a lungful of air. He wanted her to know how he felt about her. "I have to say this, because, well, because we don't know what we're facing when we get to the airstrip. And I want you to know how I feel about you."

Tears fell from her eyes. "Jase…"

"I know there are lots of things standing between us right now, including Eddie, but I love you. I love you, Reyna and I haven't said that to another woman since Abby. But I mean it, darlin'. From the bottom of my heart."

"Jase." As tears continued to stream down her face, she went back into his arms and burrowed close.

He lifted her chin and kissed her gently one more time. When he would have drawn back, ended their sweet kiss, she clung to him. He never wanted to leave her side, but if they were going to have a chance at a future together, they needed to finish the past once and for all and put it behind them.

Reluctantly, he put her away from him. "I'd better go. Stay here. Stay safe." With one final lingering glance, he left her for what he hoped would not be the last time.

He loved her. She couldn't believe she'd heard him correctly until he said it again.

She was shaking and weak from emotion. Jase *loved* her.

Reyna moved as far away from the entrance as possible. Eight minutes. The cell phone's clock said he'd been gone eight minutes. It felt like a lifetime. Her breath raced through her body at a mile a minute.

She was scared to death about her own feelings for Jase. She loved him but she'd loved Eddie, too. How could she simply move on with her life? Fall in love again as if her life with Eddie meant nothing? She owed him so much more. In a way, he'd died to protect her. She wasn't ready to let him go just yet. Would she ever be?

She glanced out the window as the storm continued to grow in intensity. What if Jase didn't come back? What if...what if he lost his life trying to protect her? Her stomach clenched in pain.

She couldn't think about that now and not rush after him.

Ten minutes passed. On an impulse that Reyna could only explain as God-led, she took the laptop bag and stuffed it as far into the crumbing fireplace as she could. There was a tiny ledge up there. She placed it on it, then hunkered down close to the ground, her eyes darting around the darkness. The place smelled dank and dusty and the walls had holes in them.

Something ran across her foot and she clamped her hand over her mouth to keep from screaming. Just a mouse. It was just a tiny little field mouse.

If she was going to keep her sanity, she needed help. She wrapped her arms tight around her body and prayed. *Lord, we need You. Please help him. Please help me.*

A noise close by drew her attention away from the prayer. She jumped to her feet and listened. Footsteps. *Footsteps.* Someone was close. Jase? No, it was too soon. She crept to the door and stopped dead in her tracks when a shadow fell across the entrance and someone blocked her way.

Two men dressed in full camouflage gear, their faces covered with ski masks, weapons drawn and pointed at her. Panic took hold and she turned on her heel to run back into the house when three more men stepped up behind her.

She started to scream, but a hand clamped over her mouth and someone whispered close to her ear, "Don't scream, Dr. Peterson." It was the man who'd threatened her at her house. *Agent Martin.*

"I'm going to take my hand away. Stay calm. This will all be over with soon. Do you understand?"

Her breath lodged in her throat. Somehow, she managed to nod and her attacker removed his hand and stepped back.

Agent Martin motioned to one of the men in front of her and he took her arm.

"It's over, Dr. Peterson. You need to come with us. Now."

FOURTEEN

Jase couldn't get the woman in the photo out of his head. Her similarity to Abby was unsettling. It was impossible, surely. Abby was dead. She had been declared so in the field even though Kyle had later told him that in the chaos that had ensued after the firefight, her body had disappeared.

Still, the CIA had later confirmed Abby's death. To do that they would have to have concrete evidence.

It was a crazy idea and it certainly didn't add up with what Jase believed he knew about her. He'd fought side by side with her. Abby was a patriot.

By the time Jase reached the landing strip, the storm had turned the sky completely dark. He stopped close to one of the hangers, his heart drumming in ears, his breath shallow. They were more than an hour late. The airstrip appeared deserted. Aaron would be gone by now but had he left word for them? He thought about Reyna. She was at the end of her strength. She couldn't go on much longer. He didn't want to have to go back and tell her they were on their own again.

"Keep her safe, Lord," he whispered under his breath.

He heard a noise close. Jase drew his weapon, his gaze panning all directions, looking for anything suspicious. Nothing.

He blew out a breath and then stepped out from behind his cover into the open. It made him feel exposed. He kept his weapon trained and continued walking, his gaze darting around each of the buildings looking for anything unusual. And then he heard the sound again. A twig breaking beneath a heavy footstep. He barely had time to turn, when the world around him flooded with blinding light.

"Drop it, Jase. It's over."

He recognized the voice. Her voice. Abby. His Abby. Abby was alive. He hadn't wanted to believe it, but now the truth was staring straight at him. His knees threatened to buckle at the realization that the woman he'd once loved had sold their entire team out for her own benefit.

His thoughts spun out of control. He couldn't seem to wrap his head around it. Abby had betrayed him in the worst possible way. An unwelcome memory surfaced about a particular incident from the past that had always bothered him. It should have made him question her allegiance back then, but he'd been blinded by love.

Jase shielded his eyes against the floodlights trained on him. The smile was the same as the woman in the photo, only the person staring back at him held little resemblance both physically and emotionally to the warm, caring person he'd once thought had loved him.

"Abby… I can't believe it. You're alive. You look… different."

"What? You don't approve of the makeover?"

She had died her hair platinum blond and something was off with the color of her eyes. They were blue. Was she wearing…contacts? That wasn't the most startling thing, though. Abby looked as if she'd aged twenty years since the last time he'd seen her. Her time on the run hadn't been kind. Her face reflected the bitterness of her heart. Standing before him now was not the woman he'd once loved, but a cold-blooded killer.

When Jase finally managed to get control of the shock and betrayal he felt, he could see Abby was standing in front of a virtual army of men. He noticed one man in particular standing next to her. His heart dropped to his feet. Kyle. No, not Kyle. He couldn't grasp it even though the reality was right before him.

Abby laughed with a sick delight when Jase realized he'd been set up. "That's right. Kyle's with our team now. It took some urging on my part. He was all set to help you as soon as he got your message. He was going to call in the full strength of the CIA to rescue you." Shrugging cavalierly, she sneered. "Naturally, I couldn't let that happen. You had to die for real this time. So I used a little...*persuasion* in the way of a carefully placed threat. He was willing to do anything I asked after that. Even find out the details of this meet."

Jase felt as if someone had slugged him in the gut. It was bad enough to be betrayed by the woman he'd once loved, but Kyle? He couldn't bear the thought. "Kyle?" Jase finally managed to choke out the words. "Is it true?"

Jase tried to read what he hoped was some hidden meaning from his friend, but nothing showed on Kyle's face. He'd couldn't believe his former handler had also sold him and Reyna out.

"How could you do it? I thought you were my friend. I trusted you." Jase stared in disbelief. It was unimaginable.

Kyle's expression was grim. "Sorry, buddy, but they threatened my sister. You know she's sick."

His friend had once told him everyone had their price. Had Kyle's price been protecting his sister?

Jase forced himself to concentrate. Where was

Aaron? No matter what Aaron had said, he didn't believe his friend would abandon them without some other way out.

Jase wasn't going to die without trying everything within his power to save Reyna. By now, she should have realized he wasn't coming back. He needed a bluff to buy her time to escape. "Well, it doesn't matter because you'll never get away with it, Abby. Reyna's on her way to the US Attorney's office as we speak."

Something Kyle said finally registered. *They threatened my sister. You know she's sick.* As far as he knew, there was nothing wrong with Emily. She was attending a university back east. Was it a message? He focused on Abby. Nothing showed on her face. She hadn't caught on.

Anger boiled inside of him at the horrible things Abby had done out of what? Greed? He lashed out. "I loved you, Abby, and you betrayed me. You betrayed our entire team for what? Money. Power. Tell why you did it. Why did the people you claimed to care about have to die so senselessly? You owe me that much at least," he demanded in a broken tone.

Abby smiled at his impassioned plea, but it didn't take away the cold from her stare. "Foolish Jase. You always did buy into that whole 'for God and country' thing. Don't you know the only person you can be loyal to is yourself? And you're wrong about Reyna. My men have her by now. She should be here any moment. Did you really think I wouldn't anticipate your next move?"

Panic swirled in his gut and made it hard to draw air into his lungs. They'd found Reyna, which meant there would be no help coming in time. He was on his own to save them.

From close behind, Jase heard the rustle of brush

and five armed men emerged. One had a firm grip on Reyna's arm.

Jase charged for them, ready to risk his life to save hers, but Abby's next words stopped him dead in his tracks. He saw the weapon pointed directed at Reyna's head. "I wouldn't, Jase. Not unless you want me to blow her brains out right now. After all, she's served her purpose. She led me to you."

The men guarding Reyna stopped a few feet away from Jase and she jerked her arm free and ran to him. One of the men tried to stop her.

"Let her go," Abby muttered. "She's not going anywhere."

Jase noticed the sheer disbelief on Reyna's face right away. She looked white as a sheet as she stared at Abby in shock.

"Sara? What are you doing here?" Reyna asked in a strangled voice. *Sara?* Jase couldn't believe it. Abby had pretended to be Reyna's friend?

His heart broke for Reyna. She had no idea the woman who claimed to be her friend was the same person responsible for Eddie's death. "Did they come after you because of me?" Reyna clasped her hand over her mouth. "Sara, I'm so sorry that I got you involved in this."

Abby stared in shock at Reyna's innocent remark.

Reyna frowned as she glanced from Abby to Jase. She could sense the tension between them, but she still didn't understand.

Then the final piece of the puzzle fell into place for Jase. He couldn't believe how brazen Abby had been to risk the chance that Reyna might recognize her through Eddie's work. After all, Reyna had seen the photo of the Scorpion team and Abby was in it. But then, when you're not expecting your best friend to be your enemy, it was easy to overlook the obvious. Just like he had with Abby.

"That's not Sara. It's Abby. My former colleague returned from the dead." Jase's mouth twisted bitterly. "She was behind the attack that killed so many of our team. Reyna, she's the one who killed Eddie."

It took a second for what he'd said to sink in. Reyna stared at him as if in a daze. She didn't want to believe it. "That can't be." She turned to face Abby. "You were my friend. We shared parts of our lives. You told me about your husband Henry's car accident. We went to the same church," she exclaimed in astonishment. "Sara, is it really is true?"

Abby shook her head at Reyna's naïveté. "I had to get close to you to find out where Eddie hid the laptop. I had a feeling he would send you to Jase. We'd been trying to eliminate *him* for years and you led us right to him. Thanks for that, by the way." Abby glanced over to where Kyle stood and then back to Jase. "Your friend here refused to give up that piece of information, but as it turned out, it wasn't necessary. We have you now. You always were a sucker for a damsel in distress. You should talk to someone about that problem, Jase. It's your Achilles' heel. Anyway, it was a smart move on Kyle's part to fake your death." She laughed nastily. "I guess there are two of us who've returned from the dead today."

"You're sick," he said in disgust.

"And you've gone soft, Bradford. When you and Reyna got away with the laptop in Eldorado and my men failed to locate you, I had to take matters into my own hands. I made Kyle an offer he couldn't refuse. His sister's life for yours."

Jase shot Kyle a look. Their eyes met. He saw something in Kyle. His friend was trying to warn him. He had to keep Abby distracted.

Jase remembered the time when the team had met with the woman who claimed to have information about the Fox. Her name was Sashi. She'd freaked when she saw Abby. Claimed Abby worked for the Fox. The team had been certain Sashi was mistaken. Especially when a few days later an alleged high ranking member of the Fox's team, a woman resembling Abby, had turned up dead.

At the time it didn't add up with what he thought knew about Abby. Now Jase realized he'd been dead wrong.

"This is because of Sashi, isn't it? She was telling the truth when she said she recognized you. What'd she do? See you with her husband arranging a weapons transfer?" At his shot in the dark, Abby's expression hardened.

"She never showed for the meet and then we were ambushed. Kyle told me they found her dead outside of her village a few days after. You killed her."

Abby looked at him in admiration. "My, my, I guess you're not as out of touch as I thought. That's right, I killed her. The entire team heard her carrying on about the Fox and me. Eventually she would have convinced someone she was telling the truth. I killed her for the same reason I killed Benjahah. They were both liabilities."

"What are you going to do when the Fox doesn't get the files you promised him?" Jase asked, and for the first time he could see he'd hit a nerve.

Her tone turned hard. "I went through a lot to get the information on the laptop. With it, I knew I could insure the Fox would rule the area with an iron fist," she said with pride. "And I would prove to be an invaluable asset to him. So killing a foolish woman like Sashi was nothing," she spat out and suddenly, her eyes darkened with anger. "Then Eddie came along. He saw me one day while he was on a mission. It was just a silly fluke."

Jase noticed Kyle kept glancing down at his watch. Was he was waiting for a signal? Reyna squeezed his arm. He believed she'd seen it, too. "How'd Eddie get your laptop?" Jase asked to keep Abby talking, and in his mind it was too big of a coincidence that Eddie's unit was in same area as the Fox. Eddie was still working for the CIA. "I take it he raided your compound. He managed to get away with the laptop."

Abby's mouth twisted into a bitter smile. "It disappeared the day before I was scheduled to meet with the Fox. All the years of clawing just to win his confidence. It was about to pay off thanks to my man in the CIA who was providing classified information." She drew an agitated breath. "But I can still fix this. Once I take care of the two of you, I'll prove myself invaluable to the Fox. And one day, I'll no longer need him at all."

"Do you really think the Fox will trust you after what Eddie accomplished? Reyna's husband made you look inept. He followed you. Found out where you were staying. Took surveillance photos. He figured out you faked your death. Eddie realized what you had planned so he took the laptop."

Abby stared into the distance as if remembering, a look of distaste on her face. "I couldn't cancel the meet. *He* would know something was wrong. I planned to stall him somehow, only when Eddie followed me there, the Fox realized we had a major breech. He told me if I didn't find a way to contain the problem, he'd get someone who could." She scowled. "My men searched everywhere but Eddie had disappeared into thin air. I knew Eddie had to die before he uncovered the identity of my contact at the CIA. He would sell me out in nothing flat, and I had gone to great lengths to eliminate anyone from my past who might eventually connect me to the Fox."

"Like Thomas and Mason. You had them killed, too. I doubt if they even knew why they died," Jase said in repulsion.

She smiled arrogantly and he shuddered at the look of pure evil on her face. "I used your affection for me to gain my position in the unit. Just as you let your Good Samaritan attitude bring you out of hiding. Now you and Reyna are going to die."

The reality of those words struck hard. Jase needed to think fast. Call her bluff. "You think so? You're wrong, Abby. You always did try to do things the easy way. Well, this time it won't work. There's another copy of the files and it's on its way to the US Attorney's office as we speak. I think they'll be interested to see the evidence in them. It's over for you. Did you really think I wouldn't have a backup plan?"

"You're lying," Abby snarled, but he could see she wasn't convinced.

"Am I? Are you willing to stake your life on it?" Jase challenged.

Somehow, she managed to recover her composure. "It doesn't matter. You'll be dead soon and I'm sure I can torture the answer out of her." She pointed her weapon at Reyna once more. "Where's the computer, Jase?" she demanded. "I need it. I promised it to the Fox over six months ago. If I can't deliver soon, it won't be good for me."

Next to him, Reyna squared her shoulders and faced Abby. "You want the computer?" Reyna asked in a hard tone. "Well, too bad, because it's not here and I'll die before I tell you where it's hidden."

Abby glared at her through narrowed eyes. "I don't believe you." She motioned to one of the men standing guard and he jerked Jase's backpack off and searched it.

The man shook his head. "It's not here."

Abby's face contorted with vehemence. "Where is it?" When Reyna didn't answer she turned her anger on Jase. "Maybe if I torture her enough you'll talk. You remember how good I am at convincing people to talk, don't you, Jase?" Abby gave him a pointed look and he knew she wouldn't hesitate to follow through with her threat.

Furious, Jase's jaw hardened and he clenched his fists at his sides. Abby would stop at nothing to get the information back. Even torturing Reyna. He couldn't let that happen. He hauled Reyna into his arms, shielding her with his body. "You'll have to kill me first," he said, his eyes blazing.

Abby simply sneered. "That certainly can be arranged." Jase could feel Reyna trembling against him as she stared at Abby. He glanced down at her expression and realized she was shaking with rage.

"You killed Eddie to save yourself?" Reyna asked in disbelief. "He was your friend. He fought beside you. Trusted you. How could you do that? What did Eddie ever do but try to help his country?" she yelled at Abby. "How could you betray your country in such a horrible way?"

To Reyna's impassioned plea, Abby appeared bored. "Are you really that naive? There is no winning this war, so why not make it profitable for me?"

Reyna lunged for Abby, but Jase grabbed her arm. Abby would kill her and not feel any remorse at all over it. She was a sociopath and Reyna would be just another obstacle standing in the way of her attaining her ultimate goal of taking over the Fox's empire.

Abby motioned to one of her men. "Take her to the office. Get the location of the laptop and the second copy out of her."

"Jase," Reyna screamed as one of the men jerked her from his arms. Jase tried to go after her, but two men grabbed him from behind.

He fought to free himself of his captors like a wild animal struggling to break free of a trap. Jase's gut burned with anger. "Let her go, Abby. Your beef is with me, not her. I'll tell you what you want to know…just let her go." He couldn't let Abby hurt Reyna. He'd die first.

Abby started to say something but before she got the words out, all around them a multitude of things began to happen. Kyle's phone chirped a single ring. Abby's attention jerked to what he was doing.

"Now," Kyle yelled, and half a dozen of the men surrounding Abby turned their weapons on her.

FIFTEEN

"Drop your weapons—all of you—if you want to live," Kyle commanded.

Abby whirled on Kyle, gun drawn. One of the men close tried to disarm her but she swung the weapon hard, knocking him out cold. Then Abby aimed the weapon at Kyle. She was going to kill him. With all his strength, Jase shoved his elbow into the gut of one of the men holding him and he released Jase and dropped to his knees. Before the second man could react, Jase slugged him hard in the chest and then he was free.

He charged for Abby. With one carefully placed swift kick, the weapon flew from her hand.

With a look bordering on admiration Abby faced him and squared off ready to do battle. He knew she was a formidable opponent. The former CIA operative had excelled in martial arts. She bounced lithely on her feet waiting to strike. Jase positioned his fists in front of him anticipating her next move. She grinned at his defensive move and charged him. She tried a round-house kick; he'd seen her use it many times to disable an enemy. Expecting it, he dodged to the right and caught her foot inches from his face. She lost her balance and fell backward onto the ground. Before Abby had time to regroup, Jase was on her and forced her arms behind her back. With Abby immobilized, he leaned over, retrieved her weapon and pointed it at her head. "Tell your men to drop their weapons. *Now*, Abby."

"Don't listen to him. Shoot them all," Abby screamed at her men.

A handful of tension-filled seconds ticked by as the standoff continued around them. And then slowly, one by one, the men dropped their weapons and raised their hands.

"Cuff them," Kyle ordered as his soldiers rushed the men and kicked their weapons away.

Jase hauled Abby to her feet and Reyna—now free— ran to his side. He pulled her close while keeping the gun trained on Abby.

"How could you betray me like this?" Abby shouted to her colleagues. "He'll kill us all."

None of her men answered. While her soldiers were being cuffed and led away, Abby turned the full weight of her anger Jase's way. "You'll never stop what's happening. You have no idea who you're dealing with. You think I'll lead you to the Fox? I won't. I'd be signing my death warrant. Without my help, you'll never figure out his identity. He's too good at staying hidden," she spit the words out.

Jase never flinched. "Sorry to disappoint you, but one of the surveillance photos Eddie took before he died is of you with a man. I'm guessing he's the Fox. With it, we can not only tie you to his organization but also identify the Fox. Thanks to you, we have our first real look at him. I'd say his days are numbered, and you, well, you're going away for a very long time."

Abby blanched and her eyes widened in terror. "Jase,

he'll kill me. You've seen what he's capable of. You have to help me," she said in a meek tone.

Jase couldn't believe she was actually trying to play on his past feelings for her.

Ignoring her, he drew Reyna closer and Abby lashed out, "He'll kill me and it'll be on your head."

"If you want my help, tell me where the Fox is hiding." It was a long shot but one he had to take. They didn't know yet what the Fox's plans were for the weapons he'd stolen or if an attack on one or all of the embassies was imminent.

Abby appeared terrified. "I can't. I'd be a dead woman."

Advancing on Abby, Kyle wasn't moved by her impassioned plea. "You did this to yourself. You caused so much harm. Took the lives of men who trusted you to have their backs. You tried to kill Reyna and Jase and you thought you could blackmail me by threatening to harm my sister."

Jase couldn't remember the last time he'd seen Kyle look so furious. "Did you really think I'd betray my country because of your threats? That text you just heard was my men letting me know Emily is safe. And for the record, my sister is perfectly healthy. I was warning Jase of the plan." Kyle waited while his words sank in.

For a second, Abby was incapable of speaking. Her sins were catching up with her at last. "You're foolish if you think you can stop the Fox, Kyle. Even if you take me and the rest of my men out of play, there'll be others to take our place. I'll never make it to Langley. I'll be dead before the chopper reaches the ground. He has that much reach."

Kyle motioned to one of the men standing close by. "Agent Booth, cuff her and get her out of my sight."

"It would be my pleasure, sir." The younger man grabbed Abby's arm and led her away.

"Do you think she'll give him up?" Kyle asked as Abby was led away. "Maybe save herself from facing a more severe punishment?"

Jase shook his head. "I doubt it. She's terrified of him."

Kyle nodded. "You're right. I'm just glad you and Reyna are okay. I'm sorry about keeping you in the dark, but once Abby thought she had me on the hook, I had to see how this played out. Too much was at stake."

Jase grinned at his friend as they watched the activity around them. "I get that now. What happened after Eddie died?" he asked curiously.

"For a while, I thought the mission was scrubbed until Abby came after me a few days ago. Then things started happening quickly. Once I received the message from your friend Aaron, I knew we had to move fast," he said with a sigh.

Jase thought about those tense moments at Aaron's house and the doubts he'd once had over Kyle's safety. "I'm just happy that you're still alive, my friend."

Kyle smiled. "Me, too. I had my second in command, Elizabeth Ramirez, loop Aaron in on what was happening. Elizabeth helped him coordinate the red tape to get the rescue mission in place so quickly. I had to make Abby believe I was cooperating by giving up the location of the meet."

Jase still couldn't fully grasp what had happened. "Unbelievable. I can't believe she was brazen enough to come after you."

"That's not the worst part. Two days ago, she had her CIA mole murdered. She was tying up loose ends.

I believe once she got the laptop, she planned to disappear and we'd never bring her or the Fox to justice."

Jase couldn't believe the things Abby was capable of. He truly had no idea what was in her heart. "Who was the mole?" he asked because he wanted to know who had helped Abby betray them.

"Sam Yarbrough, the assistant director of the science and technology division," Kyle told him, and nodded at Jase's obvious shock. "Yeah I know. It's unbelievable, isn't it?"

"Yes, it is." Jase and Reyna had been certain there was someone within the CIA aiding with the files and now they knew the name. He couldn't believe someone with the AD's power would fall prey to Abby's threats.

"What Abby didn't realize was Sam left detailed records of all the information he'd provided her for the Fox. Sam knew all about the Fox's organization. She's going away for a very long time. She may not talk, but I'm hoping one of her men will sell her out to save themselves."

"I still can't believe she betrayed her entire team for someone like the Fox," Reyna muttered in disgust.

"It's unimaginable. It was all about the fame and the power to her. She's a sociopath," Kyle said. "I'm truly sorry about Eddie. He came to me with his suspicions shortly after Jase was injured. He'd been working undercover for me since that time."

"I can't believe it. I had no idea," she managed. "Thank you for telling me."

"We had to keep it secret. I helped him get stationed in the right area to get the evidence." Sighing, Kyle glanced back over at Jase. "He knew you were still alive, brother. I told him. A few weeks before he died, Eddie reached out to me about the laptop. He said he'd put it in a safe place. He knew he couldn't give it to me because they'd be watching for any possible contact between us."

"I wish I'd known what he was going through," Reyna whispered brokenly. "Maybe I could have helped him in some way."

Jase tried to reassure her. "You did everything you could. You helped bring Eddie's killers to justice."

Kyle nodded. "That's right. Your husband worked so hard to protect the information on the laptop. Thanks to his efforts, we have Abby and her team, and hopefully we'll be able to bring down the Fox's organization once and for all. Oh, and where *is* the laptop, by the way?"

Jase turned to Reyna who said, "It's at the house where you left me. I put it in the fireplace for safe-keeping."

She never ceased to amaze him. "Smart."

Over the treetops a chopper emerged, kicking up dust and debris as it landed. "That's your friend Aaron and his team. He's been waiting for our cue to haul Abby and her goons away." Kyle hesitated and then said, "Jase, I'd like to take Abby to Defiance, to your place for the interrogation. As far as I can tell, no one beyond the men who followed Reyna knew about Defiance, and they're in custody. It might just keep her alive long enough for us to convince her to cooperate."

Kyle's request stunned him. Before he could answer, he saw Aaron disembark from the chopper followed by a tall, slender woman dressed in fatigues, her black hair pulled away from her face.

"Brother, I'm glad to see you two alive." Aaron's smile lit up his face and he clasped Jase's hand, then said to Reyna, "It's a pleasure to meet you in person, ma'am."

Reyna laughed and gave him a hug. "It's very nice to meet you, too. And it's even nicer to know that this is almost over."

"Amen to that," Aaron said with enthusiasm.

The woman beside Aaron introduced herself. "Elizabeth Ramirez. It's a pleasure to meet you, Agent Bradford. I'm glad you and Ms. Peterson made it here safely."

Jase shook the woman's hand. "Thanks, Agent Ramirez. I understand you helped coordinate this along with Aaron. We owe you both our lives."

Elizabeth humbly bowed her head. "It was a joint effort with Special Ops. We couldn't have done any of it without Aaron's help."

One of Aaron's men came over to where he stood. "We're ready to transport the prisoners, sir. The weather's deteriorating quickly. We'll need to be airborne soon."

Aaron nodded and turned back to Jase. "As much as I love a good adventure, I have to say I could use a little calm. I'm going to head out now. I'll talk to you when you arrive back in Defiance."

Aaron briefly clasped Jase's hand and gave Reyna another hug, then he and Elizabeth followed his men to the chopper.

Jase's head swam. In the course of just a few minutes, he'd discovered the woman he'd once loved was not only still alive but also the mastermind behind killing many of his friends. It was hard to wrap his head around it all. "I'd like to be part of the interrogation, if I may," he told Kyle.

His friend nodded. "Absolutely."

Reyna rubbed her hands over her arms. She was shivering from shock and from the cold but apparently unaware of it.

"You're freezing," Jase said, noticing the chill in the air. "Let's get you someplace warm."

Kyle turned to the younger man next to him. "Agent Dalton, escort Jase and Reyna to the office and have the medic meet them there to examine their injuries. I'll be there shortly. I just want to see this part of the mission through. I've waited a long time for it."

"I can understand. We'll see you when you're done." Jase was happy to let Kyle finish the job. He needed time to think clearly. Now that the threat was over, he felt like a robot going through the motions.

Reyna couldn't stop shaking. Partly from fear at what she and Jase had just gone through. They'd come so close to dying. But mostly she was just so angry at Sara's treachery.

She had trusted Sara with her secrets and with her life. She believed Sara was a friend she could trust and all along she was just using her to locate the laptop and get to Jase.

"How could she do that to Eddie?" she asked, looking up at Jase with angry tears in her eyes. "How could she do that to her own team?"

Jase appeared to be as shell-shocked as she was. "I don't know. I guess she loved the power and the money more than she loved us. Me."

Reyna could hear the pain in his voice. Learning the truth about the woman he'd once loved had to be devastating.

"I know it's wrong, but I wanted to hurt her the way she hurt Eddie. You. Me. I wanted her to feel some of our pain." Her voice broke over the words.

Jase stopped walking, grasped her firmly by the shoulders and frowned down at her. "No, Reyna, don't go there. You're not that person. You're not Abby." Of course he was right. Revenge was a wasted emotion and she wanted to put Sara's betrayal firmly behind her. With God's help she would.

A few moments later, they followed the younger agent into the office. Once inside, Jase flipped on the lights. "I can take it from here, Dalton," he told him.

"Yes, sir." Yet the young man hesitated.

"Is something wrong?" Jase asked.

"No, sir. I just wanted to say what a pleasure it is to work with you. Agent Jennings speaks very highly of you. You're a true hero."

Jase lowered his head. "Thank you, Dalton. That's nice of you to say, but Eddie Peterson's the true hero here. None of this would be possible without his efforts."

"Yes, sir." Dalton hesitated only a second longer before he left them alone.

Everything felt surreal to Reyna. She dropped down to a dusty sofa close by as if in a daze. Jase pointed to the woodstove in the corner of the office. "I'll get the fire going to take the chill from the air."

"I still can't believe it," she said without acknowledging what he'd said. "I told her all about Eddie and how tragically he'd died and she was so sympathetic when all along she was the one responsible for his death."

"She's very good at fooling people, Reyna. I believed she loved me." There was a winter chill in his voice he couldn't hide.

"I can't imagine how hard this must be for you," she said, and waited for him to say something.

The length of time it took for him to respond scared her. He stared into the fire, a hard expression on his face. "I loved her. I wanted to spend the rest of my life with her and now I realize everything between us was nothing more than a lie. It makes me think that maybe we really don't know the people we're close to after all. I mean, Eddie was still working for the CIA and you had no idea." He clenched his hands at his sides. "I can't help but think if I'd seen who the real Abby was long ago, Eddie and who knows how many others might still be alive."

"No, Jase, how could you even think that? You said yourself she was good at fooling people."

She could see he didn't believe her. With nothing left to say, a tense silence suddenly settled between them. Thankfully, the medic arrived to examine their injuries and she was spared trying to think of something to say to fill the void.

When the door opened some time later and Kyle came in, the medic was just wrapping up his examination.

"How are they holding up?" Kyle asked the man who had examined them.

"Remarkably well, considering. Thanks to Dr. Peterson's triage ability."

She managed a smile. "Thanks, but it was mostly Jase."

"Speaking of, can I steal him for a moment?" Kyle asked her.

"Of course." Reyna watched as Jase headed to the door.

"I'll only be a minute," he said without emotion. "This is almost over. Soon you'll be able to get back to your life again."

Jase stepped outside with Kyle and they walked in silence until they were a little ways from the office.

"How are you really holding up?" Kyle asked quietly.

"Honestly? Not so great." He swallowed hard. "After what just went down with Abby, I don't think I can trust anything or anyone anymore."

Kyle watched him for a long time before he spoke. "She had us all fooled. That was her intention all along. She used us to gain access to the Fox. You can't let what she did ruin what could be a very good thing for you."

Jase knew his friend was talking about Reyna, and yet his world had been turned upside down. As much as he loved her, he wasn't sure he was ready to open his heart up to that kind of hurt again. "I care about Reyna—no, I love her—but how do you trust another person after such a betrayal?"

"Jase, you should be angry, furious at what Abby did, but don't turn your back on love." Kyle clasped his shoulder. "You're blessed enough to have been given a second chance." He could see the hurt in Kyle's eyes. Was his friend thinking about the tragic way he'd lost his wife, Lena?

"I see how you look at Reyna," Kyle said. "She has that same look on her face when she looks at you. Don't let Abby destroy your chance at finding happiness again. She doesn't deserve that much power."

Jase knew his buddy was right and yet he'd need time to regroup. He was so mixed up inside right now.

"You know this is just the tip of the iceberg. It will take months if not longer to figure it all out," Kyle said in an effort to change the subject.

Jase nodded grimly. "I know."

"Which is exactly why I need you. Jase, I'm resurrecting the Scorpions and I want you to head them up once more."

For the longest time, Jase couldn't be sure he'd heard his friend correctly.

"I know it's a lot to process, but I want the Scorpions' main goal to be to dismantle the Fox's organization completely and I need honest men and women to do that. We can't afford another Abby. I want people who can't be bribed. People of integrity like you."

Jase turned back toward the office. He hadn't realized how much he missed the adrenaline rush of a mission. Bringing the bad guys down. Saving lives. He had grown weary of hiding out in his cabin alone, but would going back into the field mean he'd be letting go of any chance he had for a future with Reyna? The very thought of leaving her hurt like crazy. That had to mean something. Maybe he *was* capable of trusting again?

"I can't, Kyle. I can't go back."

"Is this because of your leg…or her?" Kyle nodded toward the office.

Jase shook his head. "I'm not fit to go back in the field. My leg would be a handicap to everyone around me."

Kyle didn't waver. "I thought you would say that, and I have a proposition for you…"

Reyna watched the door close behind him. *This is almost over. Soon you'll be able to get back to your life again.* Those words hurt so much to hear. She could feel him withdrawing from her emotionally. Almost as if seeing the woman he had once loved had changed things in his heart. Did he still love Abby in spite of everything she'd done to him? Or had her betrayal destroyed his ability to trust? Jase had told her he loved her. Had that changed?

Reyna and Jase had been so intent on figuring out who was behind the threat that she hadn't let herself think beyond the danger. Now that it had passed, where did that leave her? Where did it leave *them*?

In her heart, she knew she didn't want to let Jase go. He'd come to mean so much to her in just a short period of time. She…loved him. Was it possible to fall in love so soon? She still ached for Eddie.

All she knew was she couldn't go back to her life in Texas. Couldn't give up on a second chance at love.

She glanced up and saw Jase standing in the doorway, looking so strong and determined and handsome. He was so close and yet emotionally he appeared miles away. She could see something weighed heavy on him.

"Are you okay?" Her voice came out a breathless whisper.

Jase stepped inside and closed the door. He still had that distant look in his eyes. "Yes."

"Is something wrong?" she asked, wishing he would just say whatever it was.

He glanced away. "We're heading out now before the weather grounds us. We'll be flying back to Defiance tonight."

Somehow she managed to get the word out. "Okay." What did that mean? Was she going with him? Would she be returning home? She so desperately wanted to ask what had changed between them, but before she could work up the courage, Kyle walked in.

"Ready?" he asked both of them.

Reyna managed to nod while Jase still didn't look at her.

"Good. We need to get out of here now," Kyle said.

They followed Kyle outside. He headed for one of the choppers that was waiting to lift off and they did the same. Reyna climbed inside along with Jase and then Kyle who shut the door.

She stared out the window as the chopper struggled to lift against the roaring wind and then they were airborne. She had never felt so torn before. She still loved Eddie so much. Part of her would always love him, but Reyna had known she couldn't live in the past forever. It was time to let Eddie go and start living again.

She thought she and Jase might one day have a future together, yet the stone-silent man sitting next to her was like a stranger.

"As a precaution, I'll have my men install some extra security measures around your place including the CIA's top signal-blocking system," Kyle told Jase. "It has the capability of blocking cell signals and tracking devices for miles around. The last thing we need is to have the Fox track us to your place."

Jase nodded. "That's a good idea. I just want this to be over. We've all paid enough for the Fox's crimes."

SIXTEEN

Reyna hadn't spoken to Jase since they'd arrived at his house the day before and the place had virtually erupted with activity. Jase, along with Kyle and a dozen more agents, had disappeared into the garage behind the house and she was left alone to face her uncertain future.

She had no idea what was going on. She'd spent the time on her own, exploring the house and surrounding property.

When evening came on the second day and no one emerged with word of what was happening, Reyna went into the kitchen and made a sandwich, which she had little appetite for.

She took her plate over to the table facing the mountains. Night settled quickly in these parts. A dozen stars appeared in the sky. It was beautiful up here and peaceful, but her thoughts were in chaos.

"Lord, I need Your help. I don't know what to do. I love him, but I don't know if there's a chance for us. After all the terrible things Jase has endured, is it too much to overcome?" Tears welled up inside and spilled over and she couldn't stop then. She had wanted to believe that once they'd figured out who killed Eddie she would have some sense of peace, but nothing could be further from the truth. She hadn't expected to fall in love with Jase.

"Let's take a break," Kyle told him. Jase and Kyle stepped out of the barn. It was dark out. They'd been at it nonstop for well over twenty-four hours. Jase glanced at his watch. It was almost three in the morning.

"Why don't you go check on her," Kyle urged when he spotted him staring up at the house. "I'll keep going with Abby."

During the endless hours of trying to break Abby, one thing had become crystal clear. What he'd once felt for Abby wasn't love. He loved Reyna. He wanted the chance to have a future with *her*. Was he too late? Had he lost his one chance at true happiness because he'd had a moment of uncertainty?

Please, God, no.

Jase left Kyle to the interrogation and strode quickly to the house. He had to know how Reyna felt about him. He found her slumped against the kitchen table sleeping. She had to be exhausted. She'd been through so much. Did he have the right to ask for her heart? He was a mess and she deserved so much better.

Doubts made him turn to leave but he must have made some noise, because she awoke.

"Jase?"

He turned back to her. She was so beautiful, still half-asleep.

"Sorry, I didn't mean to wake you," he said quietly.

"It's okay. Have you found out anything yet?" she asked, covering a yawn.

When he looked at her his heart felt as if it might burst inside of him.

He came and sat down next to her. "No, nothing yet."

She stared into his eyes and suddenly she looked afraid. "But something has happened," she concluded.

He wanted to jump right in, tell her he was sorry that he'd been such a jerk, but before he could, he needed to tell her everything.

"Yes. Kyle offered me a job with the CIA." He watched her reaction closely. "He wants to resurrect the Scorpion team. Make it better. Go after the Fox full force and bring him down once and for all. He wants to honor those who lost their lives because of Abby's treason."

"That's…great. So you'll be going back on active duty. Will you be moving to Langley or overseas?" Her words came out in a rush and she started to get to her feet. He reached out and gently encircled her wrist with one hand.

"Wait. Listen to me, Reyna." She dropped back down beside him.

"I told Kyle I couldn't go back into the field again. That part of the job is over for me. Kyle was persistent and he came up with a workable alternative. He wants me to train the next group of Scorpions for duty and set up a command post where I can oversee each mission." He took a breath, exhaled slowly. "I'll be working right here in Defiance. At least until we iron all the details out. There's plenty of places on the property to set up a training facility for now. The conditions, coupled with the rugged terrain, will help with their training. I told him yes." He stopped and looked at her but she seemed incapable of responding.

"It's a chance to make the Scorpions what they started out to be. An exemplary team of agents tasked with protecting our country from outside threats. Men and women of integrity. It's a tremendous opportunity to bring something positive out of the horrendous things that happened."

"That's…wonderful." She kept her focus somewhere above his left shoulder, her hands knit together in her lap. "I'm so happy for you."

"Reyna, look at me," he said softly, and she finally did.

He took her hands in his. "I'm sorry I shut you out earlier. Seeing Abby again, learning about the dreadful things she'd done, well, it shook me. It even made me have doubts about what I know is real, like what I feel for you. Not anymore." He looked into her eyes. "I know it's too soon. You've been through so much and your head has to be spinning with everything. I know you're still grieving over Eddie. You need time. But I love you, Reyna, and I don't want to let you go. I want to marry you."

A tiny sob escaped as tears filled her eyes. "I don't want to let you go, either…and I love you, too, but you're right. It is too soon."

It hurt to hear her say she wasn't ready, but he understood.

"I have to settle things here." She pointed to her head. "I know what I feel in my heart, and I do love you, Jase, but I have to find a way to let Eddie go. When I do, will you ask me again?"

The pain he felt at hearing those words was hard to swallow, but he'd give her all the time in the world. He wanted a chance at happiness with her.

He kissed her sweetly and then let her go. "Yes. When you're ready I will ask you again. I'll be right here at my home on Defiance Mountain waiting for you. I hope you'll want to make it your home, as well."

Her tears spilled over and he dragged her into his arms and held her tight.

"Just tell me when you're ready."

EPILOGUE

Her hands shook on the steering wheel as she drove the familiar road up Defiance Mountain. Reyna couldn't help but compare how different this trip was from the other.

Back then, fear was her constant companion. Now there was only hope and the promise he'd given to her.

Spring was everywhere on the mountain. The meadows arrayed in pinks, purples and yellows. Her heart soared at the sight of them. At the possibility of the future with Jase.

He had told her he wanted her to be sure. He said when she was ready she would know and he would be right here waiting for her. She was counting on it.

Over the six months that passed since she'd seen Jase, she'd gone through an array of feelings, none of them fear. It was gone, due to the hard emotional work she'd done for herself.

When she left Colorado, she'd gone straight to Eddie's father and told him the people responsible for his son's death were in custody, thanks to Eddie's determination and Jase's bravery. Ed Sr. couldn't wait to meet the man who'd saved her life.

And he would soon.

Jase had arranged for Eddie to receive the Distin-guished Intelligence Cross, the CIA's highest decora-tion. She and Ed Sr. attended the ceremony and saw Eddie's name inscribed on the Memorial Wall at Lang-ley. She'd looked for Jase but he was standing true to his word about giving her space. He told her when she was ready he'd be waiting for her.

Reyna parked the truck and got out. Gone were all the uncertainties. Even the house looked as if it had shaken its gloomy trappings. The air was filled with the clean mountain air she'd fallen in love with. She could see living here with him. Raising their family together. She hadn't returned to Stevens. She'd extended her leave of absence. But Reyna realized she missed medicine. She'd noticed on her last time at Defiance that there was no medical facility close by. She planned to open one soon. Maybe specialize in pediatric medicine.

Right now she was ready. Ready for love. Ready for Jase. She took out her phone and typed the message she hoped he was still waiting to hear.

I'm ready...

Jase had been sitting inside his office staring out a perfect spring day when her text message came in.

He almost dropped the phone. He'd waited through some of the worst six months of his life to hear those words. Yet, through it all, he hadn't once given up hope, trusting God and Reyna. He'd stepped out on the faith that she would return his love one day and he'd found his mother's wedding ring. Jase kept it on his desk to remind him of what waited for him.

There was more to life than dealing with the dark depths of the human heart. The team had made great strides in finding and eliminating some of the routes the Fox used to transport his weapons from Afghanistan. They'd posted photos of the man they believed to be the Fox everywhere with a reward for his capture. There had been thousands of leads. So far, none had produced the terrorist but the Fox was on the run and Jase was hopeful. With the information Eddie had provided, he believed it was only a matter of time before they broke the backbone of the Fox's organization.

Jase had spent a horrific three months of his life trying to break Abby and her team. In the end, they were more afraid of the Fox's vengeance than charges of treason. Kyle had arranged the transfer to bring them to Langley. The chopper never made it. The Fox's reach had been long, indeed. They'd discovered too late that the Fox implanted tracking chips in all his soldiers. Abby hadn't been any different. When she didn't show up with the laptop, the Fox had begun searching for her. He probably suspected she'd been captured by her former employer. Because of the signal-blocking system Kyle had put in place at Jase's house, he hadn't been able to locate her until they were in public airspace. Then he'd eliminated her and her men.

For the longest time, Jase couldn't have been more discouraged. He felt as if he'd somehow let Abby down, but as Kyle was quick to point out, she had chosen her own path in life. Her death lay squarely at her own feet.

On the bright side, Aaron had signed on to assist with the training and had suggested they move the training camp to Don and Linda's place. Jase was surprised but as it turned out the older couple was thrilled at the prospect of being able to stay in the home they loved and at having young people around once more.

Now, all of Jase's worries evaporated. There was more to life than death. There was Reyna and the future.

Where are you? he texted. He so desperately wanted to see her.

Look in your driveway...

She was here in Defiance. He tucked the ring into his pocket and hurried toward the front of the house. He threw open the door and there she was, standing next to a U-Haul. He laughed as he imagined this petite woman driving such a huge truck.

Jase descended the steps as if he floated over them, until he stood next to her.

"Hi," she said, and she was smiling. His heart soared. She was so beautiful standing there with a tremulous smile on her lovely face. Her long, golden-brown hair was ruffled by the wind. He wanted to kiss her so bad, but he needed to be sure. Needed her to be, too. "Does this mean...?"

"I'm ready. To move to Defiance." His heart plummeted and she saw it. "And to marry you. I want to marry you, Jase. Now...well, as soon as we can arrange it. I want to move forward. I want—" She didn't get the chance to finish because he took her in his arms and kissed her as he'd dreamed of for so long. She melted against him, returning his passionate kiss with all her heart.

He wanted the kiss to go on forever. He'd missed her so much, but she pulled away and he let her go. He stared down at her face. She'd suddenly gone serious.

"You were right. As hard as it was to hear, you were right. I wasn't ready. I was still holding on to the past. Eddie. The life we had once shared." She smiled up at him. "I'm ready now."

Thank You, God, he recited to himself. God had granted him the desires of his heart and he'd be eternally grateful.

He stroked her cheek. "I'm so glad."

She stared off at the distant mountain peak still covered in snow. "I was holding on to my grief like a lifeline. I still have Eddie's ashes," she confessed, and looked at him, trying to gauge his reaction. "I guess I thought as long as I had them I could keep him close. He wouldn't want that. I brought him here with me. Eddie always wanted to see Colorado. I'm hoping you can help me find the right place to scatter them."

Tears had filled her eyes. He realized how hard letting go of Eddie was for her.

"Of course. I have the perfect spot." And he did. A little meadow at the base of the mountain. It was private, and close enough that they could both go there to visit Eddie any time they wanted. Right now it would be covered it wildflowers. He believed it would do Eddie justice.

"There's something else you should know," she said, and the strain in her tone caught his attention. Was she still having doubts?

"Please tell me you're not having second thoughts." His heart thudded against his chest. He wanted her, but he wanted all of her.

"No," she rushed to assure him. "Of course not." She wrapped her arms around his waist and drew him closer. He looked into her eyes and saw that was true. "No, Jase. I want you. I want to be your wife. I want to have your children."

He buried his face against his neck. He could smell the fragrance of her skin as she held him tight. "Thank you."

When his heart stopped throbbing in his chest, he re-membered there was more to say and so he let her go. "Sorry, it's just that I've dreamed of this moment for so long."

She smiled through her tears. "Me, too. What I wanted to tell you was that I've bought a house in Defiance."

This was the last thing he expected. He'd been so wrapped up in trying to determine the Fox's next move without the much-needed intel from Abby that he and his team had been locked away on this mountain for months. He hadn't so much as gone into town for a cup of coffee and to catch up on the local news at Maggie's.

"Why?" he asked in surprise.

At his baffled expression, she added, "I plan to live there until we're married and then I'm giving the house to Eddie's father. I want him close. He's my family and he needs me."

Relief threatened to collapse his legs. He respected her loyalty to Eddie's father.

"He'll love you, Jase. I've told him everything about you. How you helped bring Eddie's killers to justice. He's anxious to meet you."

Jase was honored to have the man as part of their family. There was just one thing left to do. She was a special woman and she needed a proper proposal. He wanted to do this right.

He took the ring from his pocket and dropped to one knee and held it out to her. A sob escaped when she saw it and she covered her mouth with her hands, staring at him in wonderment.

"Reyna Peterson, I love you with every breath I take. Will you do me the honor of becoming my wife?"

As her tears fell from her eyes, she somehow man-aged a nod.

He slipped the ring onto her finger and smiled at her happiness. "Is that a yes?"

"Yes, oh yes," she whispered. "It's beautiful, Jase."

"It belonged to my mom. It's been in our family for years. It suits you," he said, and then wrapped his arms around her waist and hugged her close.

She kissed the top of his head before drawing him to his feet. "I love that it's part of your family's history. I love you. And I can't wait to be your wife."

* * * * *

Dear Reader,

There's just something about the mountains that gets in your blood. If you've ever taken a walk in them, you'll understand. Maybe it's the breathtaking views, the clean mountain air, or the fact that God's majesty can be seen everywhere you look.

That is why I chose the rugged Rocky Mountains as the backdrop for my latest Love Inspired Suspense novel.

In *Rocky Mountain Pursuit*, a mystery that started years earlier in the dry deserts of Afghanistan will finally be unveiled. I love the contrast between the barren desert and the mountains bursting with life. It reminds me of what God does for us. He brings us out of the desert to abundant life. We just have to trust Him.

In *Rocky Mountain Pursuit*, former CIA Agent Jase Bradford and Reyna Peterson risk everything to discover the truth about what happened in the desert three years earlier. To save their own lives, they must find out who was responsible for the attack that almost destroyed Jase's entire Scorpion team and ultimately cost Reyna's husband his life. The surprising answer will finally be revealed on the snowy mountains of Colorado. And, with God's perfect timing, Jase and Reyna will be able to put their dark pasts behind them and rebuild their lives…together.

When we're in the middle of our own storm, it's hard to remember that God's timing is indeed perfect. Waiting for answers can be so hard, but if we wait on God, He will bring us out of any storm. Just as He did with Jase and Reyna.

All the best…
Mary Alford

COMING NEXT MONTH FROM
Love Inspired® Suspense

Available March 1, 2016

NO ONE TO TRUST • by Melody Carlson
After Jon Wilson is injured while rescuing Leah Hampton from an attacker on the beach, they run for their lives. Now, as they encounter danger around every corner, they must uncover why someone wants them dead.

PROTECTING HER DAUGHTER
Wrangler's Corner • by Lynette Eason
Someone is trying to kidnap Zoe Collier's daughter, Sophia, and she will risk anything to keep her child safe. And Aaron Starke, the veterinarian she met while in hiding, is determined to do the same.

MISTAKEN TARGET • by Sharon Dunn
Hiding out at an island resort after his cover is blown, FBI informant Diego Cruz is forced to flee with Samantha Jones when an assassin, confusing their cabins, inadvertently attacks Samantha instead of him.

COVERT CARGO
Navy SEAL Defenders • by Elisabeth Rees
When Beth Forrester finds a terrified child wandering next to her lighthouse, she unwittingly becomes the target of a Mexican cartel. And only Dillon Randall, an undercover navy SEAL, can save her.

SUDDEN RECALL • by Lisa Phillips
CIA agent Sienna Cartwright's last mission left her with amnesia. So she turns to her former boyfriend Deputy US Marshal Jackson Parker as she tries to regain her memories...and stay ahead of the people who want to make sure she never remembers her past.

LAST STAND RANCH • by Jenna Night
When Olivia Dillon retreats to a family ranch after making a powerful enemy, trouble follows her. And she must depend on Elijah Morales—a neighboring rancher and former army ranger—for protection.

LISCNM0216

REQUEST YOUR FREE BOOKS!

2 FREE RIVETING INSPIRATIONAL NOVELS
PLUS 2 FREE MYSTERY GIFTS

Love Inspired
SUSPENSE
RIVETING INSPIRATIONAL ROMANCE

YES! Please send me 2 FREE Love Inspired® Suspense novels and my 2 FREE mystery gifts (gifts are worth about $10). After receiving them, if I don't wish to receive any more books, I can return the shipping statement marked "cancel." If I don't cancel, I will receive 4 brand-new novels every month and be billed just $4.99 per book in the U.S. or $5.49 per book in Canada. That's a savings of at least 17% off the cover price. It's quite a bargain! Shipping and handling is just 50¢ per book in the U.S. and 75¢ per book in Canada.* I understand that accepting the 2 free books and gifts places me under no obligation to buy anything. I can always return a shipment and cancel at any time. Even if I never buy another book, the two free books and gifts are mine to keep forever.

123/323 IDN GH5Z

Name _____ (PLEASE PRINT)

Address _____ Apt. #

City _____ State/Prov. _____ Zip/Postal Code

Signature (if under 18, a parent or guardian must sign)

Mail to the **Reader Service:**
IN U.S.A.: P.O. Box 1867, Buffalo, NY 14240-1867
IN CANADA: P.O. Box 609, Fort Erie, Ontario L2A 5X3

**Are you a current subscriber to Love Inspired® Suspense books
and want to receive the larger-print edition?
Call 1-800-873-8635 or visit www.ReaderService.com.**

LIS15

SPECIAL EXCERPT FROM

Love Inspired
SUSPENSE

*With a dirty cop out to silence them forever, strangers
Leah Hampton and Jon Wilson must depend on each
other to survive.*

Read on for a sneak preview of
NO ONE TO TRUST
by **Melody Carlson**.

Leah Hampton felt her stomach knot as she watched the
uniformed officer in her rearview mirror. His plump
face appeared flushed and slightly irritated in the late
afternoon sun. Glancing around the deserted dune area,
as if worried someone else was around, he adjusted his
dark glasses and sauntered up to her old Subaru. She'd
noticed the unmarked car several miles back but hadn't
been concerned. She hadn't been speeding on this
isolated stretch of beach road—her car's worn shocks
couldn't take it.

Getting out of her car, she adjusted her running tank and
smoothed her running shorts, forcing an optimistic smile.
"Hello," she said in a friendly tone. "I was just heading
out for a beach run. Is something wrong, Officer?"

"Is that your car?"

"Yep." She nodded at her old beater. "And I know I
wasn't speeding."

"No…" He slowly glanced over his shoulder again.
What was he looking for? "You weren't speeding."

"So what's up?" She looked around, too. "Is there

some kind of danger out here? I mean, I do get a little concerned about jogging alone this time of day, especially down here where there's no phone connectivity. But I love this part of the beach, and I'm training for the Portland marathon and it's hard to get my running time in."

"You'll need to come with me," he said abruptly.

"Come with you?" She stared into the lenses of his dark sunglasses, trying to see the eyes behind them, but only the double image of her own puzzled face reflected back at her. "Why?"

"Because I have a warrant for your arrest."

"But you haven't even checked my ID. You don't know who I am." She held up her wallet, but before she could remove her driver's license, he smacked her hand, sending the wallet spilling to the ground.

"Doesn't matter who you are," he growled, "not where you're going."

Don't miss
NO ONE TO TRUST by Melody Carlson,
available March 2016 wherever
Love Inspired® Suspense books and ebooks are sold.

www.LoveInspired.com